PRAISE FOR

The Girl in the Flammable Skirt:

"Bender's taut prose works its wise melodies throughout this first collection . . . Each short story packs a heavy punch, and each should be savored. From cleverly comic to starkly surreal, Bender's audacious characters surprise and delight. Sometimes, they even make you weep."

—*Boston Globe*

"Bender's world is strange and fabulous, an ultravivid, matter-of-fact presentation of extraordinary circumstances and bizarre fulfillments . . . Declarative and telegraphic, Bender's stories read like modern fables—with a healthy sense of twisted humor thrown in for good measure."

—*Village Voice Literary Supplement*

"A wild imagination, full of bikini-bold sexiness and brute deformity, shaped into art by the sure hand of a fabulist."

—*Philadelphia Inquirer,* Best Fiction of 1998

"As Bender explores a spectrum of human relationships, her perfectly pitched, shapely writing blurs the lines between prose and poetry. While full of funny moments, these tales are neither slight nor glib . . . Bender's is a unique and compassionate voice, and her debut is a string of jewels."

—*Publishers Weekly* (starred review)

"The unexpected is ever present with startling clarity in Bender's first collection of provocative tales."

—*Library Journal*

"You don't know weird until you've read this original, at times borderline-absurd short story collection."

—*Mademoiselle*

"These stories plumb and expose deep tensions hidden in the mundane."

—*Washington Post*

"These stories, so often surreal, achieve a persistent, unnerving brilliance—they capture and render a mind's outer limits in such a way that the reader keeps nodding, sometimes reluctantly, in acknowledgment of the justice done to the mind's huge capacity for reverie, for fantasy."

—Robert Coles

"What hilarious, sweet, sexy stories Aimee Bender has dreamed up! With effortless audacity, in progressions as natural as breathing and inevitable as the world's hard surprises, she unnerves the reader in ways that remind me of the awful comic gravity of Kafka and the Brothers Grimm."

—Geoffrey Wolff

"Aimee Bender's stories come as a revelation, outlandish and fresh and disarming, as visionary as Bruno Schulz or Angela Carter, but startlingly contemporary and close to home, a voice that dances in the precipices even as it aches with the weight of the world. She's a thrilling discovery."

—Jonathan Lethem

THE GIRL IN THE

FLAMMABLE SKIRT

stories by *Aimee Bender*

ANCHOR BOOKS
A DIVISION OF RANDOM HOUSE, INC.
New York

FOR MY MOTHER AND FATHER

FIRST ANCHOR BOOKS EDITION, SEPTEMBER 1999

The following stories appeared previously and are reprinted by permission of
the author: "The Rememberer" in the *Missouri Review* (Fall 1997); "Call My
Name" in the *North American Review* (Spring 1998); "What You Left in the
Ditch" in *The Antioch Review* (Fall 1997); "Quiet Please" in *GQ* (May
1998); "Skinless" (under the title "Erasing") in the *Colorado Review* (Spring
1996); "Fugue" in *Absolute Disaster/Santa Monica Review* (Spring 1997); "Fell
This Girl" in *Faultline* (Fall 1997); "The Healer" in *Story* (Winter 1998);
"Loser" in *Granta* (Winter 1998); "Legacy" in *Cream City Review* (Spring
1997); "Dreaming in Polish" in *Threepenny Review* (Spring 1995); "The
Ring" in the *Massachusetts Review* (Fall 1997).

The Library of Congress has cataloged the hardcover edition of this work
as follows:
Bender, Aimee.
   The girl in the flammable skirt: stories / by Aimee Bender.—
1st ed.
      p.   cm.
   1. United States—Social life and customs—20th century—Fiction.
I. Title.
PS3552.E538447G57   1998
813'.54—dc21   97-44485
                                                              CIP

ISBN 0-385-49216-2

www.anchorbooks.com

Printed in the United States of America
10 9 8 7 6 5 4 3

CONTENTS

PART ONE

THE REMEMBERER

My lover is experiencing reverse evolution. I tell no one. I don't know how it happened, only that one day he was my lover and the next he was some kind of ape. It's been a month and now he's a sea turtle.

I keep him on the counter, in a glass baking pan filled with salt water.

"Ben," I say to his small protruding head, "can you understand me?" and he stares with eyes like little droplets of tar and I drip tears into the pan, a sea of me.

He is shedding a million years a day. I am no scientist, but this is roughly what I figured out. I went to the old biology teacher at the community college and asked him for an approximate time line of our evolution. He was irritated at first—he wanted money. I told him I'd be happy to pay and then he cheered up quite a bit. I can hardly read his time

3

line—he should've typed it—and it turns out to be wrong. According to him, the whole process should take about a year, but from the way things are going, I think we have less than a month left.

At first, people called on the phone and asked me where was Ben. Why wasn't he at work? Why did he miss his lunch date with those clients? His out-of-print special-ordered book on civilization had arrived at the bookstore, would he please pick it up? I told them he was sick, a strange sickness, and to please stop calling. The stranger thing was, they did. They stopped calling. After a week, the phone was silent and Ben, the baboon, sat in a corner by the window, wrapped up in drapery, chattering to himself.

Last day I saw him human, he was sad about the world.

This was not unusual. He was always sad about the world. It was a large reason why I loved him. We'd sit together and be sad and think about being sad and sometimes discuss sadness.

On his last human day, he said, "Annie, don't you see? We're all getting too smart. Our brains are just getting bigger and bigger, and the world dries up and dies when there's too much thought and not enough heart."

He looked at me pointedly, blue eyes unwavering. "Like us, Annie," he said. "We think far too much."

I sat down. I remembered how the first time we had sex, I left the lights on, kept my eyes wide open, and concentrated really hard on letting go; then I noticed that his eyes were open too and in the middle of everything we sat down on the floor and had an hour-long conversation about poetry. It was all very peculiar. It was all very familiar.

Another time he woke me up in the middle of the night, lifted me off the pale blue sheets, led me outside to the stars and whispered: *Look, Annie, look—there is no space for anything but dreaming*. I listened, sleepily, wandered back to bed and found myself wide awake, staring at the ceiling, unable to dream at all. Ben fell asleep right away, but I crept back outside. I tried to dream up to the stars, but I didn't know how to do that. I tried to find a star no one in all of history had ever wished on before, and wondered what would happen if I did.

On his last human day, he put his head in his hands and sighed and I stood up and kissed the entire back of his neck, covered that flesh, made wishes there because I knew no woman had ever been so thorough, had ever kissed his every inch of skin. I coated him. What did I wish for? I wished for good. That's all. Just good. My wishes became generalized long ago, in childhood; I learned quick the consequence of wishing specific.

I took him in my arms and made love to him, my sad man. "See, we're not thinking," I whispered into his ear while he kissed my neck, "we're not thinking at all" and he pressed his head into my shoulder and held me tighter. Afterward, we went outside again; there was no moon and the night was dark. He said he hated talking and just wanted to look into my eyes and tell me things that way. I let him and it made my skin lift, the things in his look. Then he told me he wanted to sleep outside for some reason and in the morning when I woke up in bed, I looked out to the patio and there was an ape sprawled on the cement, great furry arms covering his head to block out the glare of the sun.

Even before I saw the eyes, I knew it was him. And once we were face to face, he gave me his same sad look and I hugged those enormous shoulders. I didn't even really care, then, not at first, I didn't panic and call 911. I sat with him outside and smoothed the fur on the back of his hand. When he reached for me, I said No, loudly, and he seemed to understand and pulled back. I have limits here.

We sat on the lawn together and ripped up the grass. I didn't miss human Ben right away; I wanted to meet the ape too, to take care of my lover like a son, a pet; I wanted to know him every possible way but I didn't realize he wasn't coming back.

Now I come home from work and look for his regular-size shape walking and worrying and realize, over and over, that he's gone. I pace the halls. I chew whole packs of gum in mere minutes. I review my memories and make sure they're still intact because if he's not here, then it is my job to remember. I think of the way he wrapped his arms around my back and held me so tight it made me nervous and the way his breath felt in my ear: right.

When I go to the kitchen, I peer in the glass and see he's some kind of salamander now. He's small.

"Ben," I whisper, "do you remember me? Do you remember?"

His eyes roll up in his head and I dribble honey into the water. He used to love honey. He licks at it and then swims to the other end of the pan.

This is the limit of my limits: here it is. You don't ever know for sure where it is and then you bump against it and bam, you're there. Because I cannot bear to look down into the water and not be able to find him at all, to search the tiny clear waves with a microscope lens and to locate my lover, the one-celled wonder, bloated and bordered, brainless, benign, heading clear and small like an eye-floater into nothingness.

I put him in the passenger seat of the car, and drive him to the beach. Walking down the sand, I nod at people on towels, laying their bodies out to the sun and wishing. At the water's edge, I stoop down and place the whole pan on the tip of a baby wave. It floats well, a cooking boat, for someone to find washed up on shore and to make cookies in, a lucky catch for a poor soul with all the ingredients but no container.

Ben the salamander swims out. I wave to the water with both arms, big enough for him to see if he looks back.

I turn around and walk back to the car.

Sometimes I think he'll wash up on shore. A naked man with a startled look. Who has been to history and back. I keep my eyes on the newspaper. I make sure my phone number is listed. I walk around the block at night in case he doesn't quite remember which house it is. I feed the birds outside and sometimes before I put my one self to bed, I place my hands around my skull to see if it's growing, and wonder what, of any use, would fill it if it did.

CALL MY NAME

I'm spending the afternoon auditioning men.

They don't know it. This is a secret audition, come as you are.

"No really," I say to the beanpole man on the Muni with eyes so tired you can see death lounging in them already, "do you prefer cats or dogs?"

He smiles at me in this tolerant way. I can't tell you exactly what I'm looking for, but I'll know it when it happens. I want to be breathless and weak, crumpled by the entrance of another person inside my soul. I want to be violated by insight.

"Cats, no question," he says, pill-rolling with his fingers. He's drugged out, but I don't care. What I care about is dogs, and I am disappointed.

I thank him, run a hand through my hair and go back to

sitting at my surveillance spot, front row, facing backward, right behind the driver who winked at me when I came on.

I wear dresses on the subway. I have a lot of money from my dead father who invented the adhesive wall hook. He invented it when he was in his twenties and the world scrambled, doe-eyed, to his doorstep—no one cares for nails anymore. He died when I was three so I never really knew him enough to miss him and there are millions of dollars for me and my mom, and she isn't a spender. So it's just me! It's all me! I don't much like expensive cars or gourmet dinners; what I love are fancy dresses. Today I am wearing maroon satin, a floor-length dress with a V back and matching sandals with crisscross straps up my ankles. My ears are lit by simple diamond earrings. I look like I should know how to waltz, and I do.

The men are pleased when I come on the subway because I am the type who usually drives her own car. I am not your average subway girl, wearing black pants and reading a novel the whole time so you can't even get eye contact. Me, I look at them and smile at them and they love it. I bet they talk about me at the dinner table—I give boring people something to discuss over corn.

The beanpole man stands up to exit and nods to me. I wiggle my fingers, bye. His death eyes crinkle up in a wise way and I almost want to chase after him, have him look down on me with that look and tell me something brilliant about myself, unveil my whole me with one shining sentence, but there's really no point. He couldn't do it. His eyes crinkle up because he's been in the sun too much—he doesn't even know my name.

I think I'm done, that I've checked out the whole car, when I see that behind the older woman in the dull beige suit who keeps trying to sleep, there is someone I didn't notice before. The shy man. He is leaning against the window, wanting a cigarette and not looking at me. I go sit down right next to him.

"If you smoke out the window," I tell him in a low voice, "no one will notice."

"What?" He's about ten years older than I am, and his eyes are bright, watery even.

"I won't tell if you smoke."

He gets it and blinks. "Thanks," he says, but he doesn't move.

My dress is slithering all over the orange plastic seat, sounding like a holiday.

"So, what's your name?" I ask.

He has his head looking out the window, watching the dark cement flash by. The back of his hair is matted down, like he's just woken up from a nap.

"Or where are you going?" I say louder.

He turns to me, eyebrows up.

I lean in a little. My hair falls forward and I can smell my shampoo which smells like almonds. "I'm just curious," I say. "What stop?"

"Powell," he says. "Your hair smells like almonds."

I'm so pleased he noticed.

"Do you prefer dogs or cats?" I ask him, even though I don't really, at this exact second, need to know.

"You ask a lot of questions," he says.

"Yes."

"Well."

"What?" My dress isn't holding to the seat, I could slide right down to the floor.

"I prefer," he says, "whichever turns around when you call its name."

He may be shy but he looks me in the eye the whole time.

The train strains to a stop and he stands up to slide past me. But I'm up with him. The bottom of my dress is dusty from the floor of the subway and I'm thinking it looks sort of vintage that way. He presses on the handle and he's out the door really fast, and I just barely have a moment to look at the car I've been surveying and watch the people watch me exit. A man with a briefcase smiles back but the women all ignore me.

I float behind the shy man for a few blocks; he's up the escalator and onto Market Street and doesn't notice my burgundy shadow behind him until he ducks into a retail shoe store and then I'm hard to miss. The salesgirls are on me in one second, I have Purchase written all over me. So they think. This is a lame shoe store.

"Hey," says the man, "you following me?"

"May-be." I saunter over to a pair of shoes and pick them up even though they're so ugly and poorly made.

"Those are one of our best sellers," says salesgirl number one who has lipstick on her front tooth.

"That is not a good selling point for me," I tell her, "and you have lipstick on your tooth."

Her head ducks down and she rubs her forefinger on it. "Thanks," she says in a quiet whisper, like it's a secret, "I hate that."

The man has left the store—one second of conversation with a stupid salesgirl on my stupid part, and he's gone. The store owner is behind the counter watching me glance around at the racks of shoes and he tilts his head, indicating the staircase behind him.

"You his girlfriend?" he says.

"Maybe," I say again. Really: if the shy man didn't care at all, if he hadn't looked at me with a certain sly hunger then I wouldn't be here. But he was half there with me, I saw him thinking about the heavy sound the satin would make piled on his floor, I saw him wondering. He may have wondered very quietly, but that still counts.

I thank the store manager by placing one solid hand on his shoulder and squeezing it. Maybe someday I'll come in here and buy fourteen pairs of shoes from him. Not like I'd wear them, but I could go give them to homeless people who must like a change every now and then. I'll buy practical shoes, cushioned soles, no heels or anything. You probably walk a lot when you're homeless so heels would not be a good choice.

The staircase is fairly dark but you can still sense the glare of the daylight outside so it doesn't feel scary, just cool and slightly musty. Luckily, there's only one apartment at the top of the staircase. I try the door and it's open. For me, it's more nerve-wracking to knock than to just go on in. He's sitting in his living room with a beer and no shirt, watching TV. He looks at me, sort of amused, not really surprised.

"Persistent dress lady," he says, "you are one persistent cookie."

I love being called cookie. I love it. I love it.

I go to sit next to him on the couch.

"Do you know how to waltz?" I ask.

He flips a few channels and then turns off the TV. "So what's the deal?" he says. "Are you a prostitute?"

The thing is, I'm not offended. This makes me feel like he's getting the sexual vibe which makes me feel good, you know, alive.

"No," I say. "I just like you. Do you have plans tonight? It's Friday night, maybe we can do something."

"I have plans tonight," he says. He looks at his watch. "It's two o'clock. In six hours."

His chest is tan and a little bit doughy, soft nipples that look like a woman's. For some reason it's hard for me to even look at those nipples. They look so fragile, like fruit pulp waiting to be cut into wedges and served up in an exotic kiwi salad. It makes me want to crawl on top of him and put my thumbs on his soft fruity nipples and press down on them hard like they're elevator buttons: hey, baby, take me to a higher floor. I wonder if he's feeling lucky, I mean how often does a beautiful girl follow you home and come into your house? That's lucky. That's what guys wish for.

"So." He leans back on his couch and grabs a cigarette from the side table. I knew it. "I suppose I'd like to cut that dress right off of you."

"Really?"

"Yup." He takes a long drag off his cigarette and then stubs it out. Maybe I should be scared, but I'm not. There's the sound of all the cars and buses going by on Market Street, and it reassures me.

"Knife or scissors?"

He smiles. "Knife," he says.

"I don't know," I say, "that's a little much, I think, for me."

"Scissors." He relights the butt in the ashtray and smokes it again.

"Okay. Scissors."

"You can let go of that incredible dress as easy as that?" he asks.

"I can." I have a bank account the size of your apartment, I'm thinking. I can see, on his bathroom door, an adhesive hook holding up a black T-shirt.

He goes to his bedroom and comes out with a pair of orange-handled scissors. He walks slowly even though he knows I'm watching him. Back on the couch, he doesn't sit any closer to me but just takes the hem and slices up, up past my hip, waist, side of my breast, under my arm, down the sleeve, up around, to the shoulder, snip at the neck. I feel like he took a letter opener and gently opened me up; he did such a neat job of it. Leaning back on his side of the couch, he replaces the scissors and surveys his work. I smile at him. The next move should be his.

"I don't think I'm going to touch you," he says.

I'm there, waiting, body cooled by the breeze coming in off the street through the window behind us.

"What?" I know he can see my breast; it's right there; I can sense it out of the bottom of my eye.

"Nope." He stands up and looks around.

"What, are you going to tie me up or something?" I slide out my other arm so that my upper body is exposed, just my legs and waist still swathed in maroon satin. His couch is kelly green and it's an interesting contrast. I spend a minute appreciating this.

"Tie you up?" He goes to the refrigerator and pours himself a glass of water. "No. I don't do that shit." He doesn't seem to even notice that I'm half out of the dress.

"Hello," I say, "what is going on here? You just opened up my dress."

"Yeah," he says, "thanks."

"But we have six hours," I tell him, "you said we have six hours."

"Well," he says, sipping the water, the counter between us, "what would you like to do?"

I'm up off the couch which means the dress is on the floor and I'm naked in high heels. Which is maybe how I've

16

wanted to be all day, those straps crisscrossing up my ankles like painted snakes. I take the water out of his hand and hop up on the kitchen counter and pull him to me with my feet. Then I kiss him, smoke taste still on his lips which are cold from the water. He keeps his mouth closed and I press my body to his. "Six hours," I say, "is a long time."

"Lady," he says, "I don't think it's going to happen here. I wanted to cut your dress. I don't really want to fuck you, that's just not what I'm looking for today. Sorry if that was misleading."

He has his water back in his hand. I take it from him and have a sip. It's just water.

"Yeah, well," I tell him, "it was. I do think cutting up someone's dress is misleading."

Stepping back, he exits my feet without difficulty, and looks straight at me, into me, like he did in the subway, the way that I love. He leans against the refrigerator and a magnet drops to the floor.

"You want to be tied up?" he says then. "I'll tie you up."

If I need to scream, out of the millions of people on Market Street, one of them will hear me. Someone would hear me and do something. I can scream really, really loud.

He leads me to his bedroom which is very plain, nothing on the walls, an unmade bed. He has one chair at a desk and he puts me in it and goes to his closet and removes two belts. He starts to weave one of the belts through the slats at the back of the chair and around my hands.

"Bedroom or living room?" he asks, his voice sort of flat.

17

"Living room, please," I say.

Lifting me up in the chair, he brings me into the other room. My arms are already bound so he begins on my legs with swift, efficient hands. The window is still open, and I'm thinking about where I should aim my scream just in case.

It seems like he can't tie both legs effectively without another belt so he reaches down and whips the one out of his jeans, which then sink a little lower on his hips. I can see the broken angle of his pelvis. His nipples are still soft. I lean down, feeling like a deer in a trap, and dare to kiss one of them, bite it a little, those sweet soft fearful nipples.

"Hey," he says, "I'm doing something here."

I lean forward to try to kiss him again but he has stepped back, and I can't move. He circles the chair and tests the belts. I arch my back. My breasts are poking out like cones, my nipples are not soft. He goes to the couch and turns on the TV.

"You go imagine what you want," he says, "tell me when you want to be untied."

I jump the chair around some so that I can see him.

"What do you mean?" I say. He sticks his feet up on the coffee table, and starts to gently fold my dress.

"Just what I said."

"You tie me up just to tie me up?"

He puts the dress in a neat pile next to him, and runs a hand through his hair again. Why does everyone but me look so fucking tired? I get too much sleep. He takes a deep breath. "For right now," he says steadily, "I'm going to watch TV."

I watch with him for a minute; it's a show about Mozart. But I can't really concentrate because behind the TV is the bathroom door with the hook and I can't stop looking at that. My father was a millionaire, I want to tell him. You can't just tie up a millionaire's daughter and not fuck her. You can't just tie her up while she's naked with maroon sandals strapping her ankles and a taut stomach from ten million sit-ups and watch television! Who do you think you are?

I want to jump the chair over and pounce on him, but I can't steer it very well, so instead I turn my head around and stare at him, first seductively and then like a pain in the ass.

He looks up after a while. "Yes?"

"I'm bored," I say.

"You want to go home now?"

"But we have six hours." It comes out sounding whiny. I wait for him to react, but he doesn't tell me to shut up and then unbuckle his pants with one quick rip. His face is kind, still tired, cheeks slack. I want to lay his head on my chest and soothe him, poor man who lives alone in this shitty apartment. Poor man. Let me love you here on your green couch for the street to see, let me offer you something magical in the space between my breasts. Please. Please. Let me.

"Lady," he says again, "you ready to go home?"

I'm thinking about the walk home. I'll have to go into one of the stores and buy myself another dress. I'll borrow one of his T-shirts, or if he doesn't let me, then I'll wrap the satin around me like a towel. The salesgirl will note the strange outfit but acknowledge the fineness of the material, and decide I'm a good bet. She'll tell me her name and hang up my choices while I still browse around. Maybe I'll tell her the story of this dress, but leave it open-ended. And she'll giggle, for after all, I am the customer. I'll take a cab home in a new glorious brocade cream-colored gown. My apartment is big and I have a big TV. I have a velvet couch and it's one of a kind. I have cable. I have better reception than this stupid nipple man. I have a remote control that can work through walls.

I look at him again; he's lighting up another match to continue smoking that same first cigarette.

"No," I tell him, slumping back down in the chair. "I don't want to go home yet." He turns to look at me. "Is that okay?" I ask.

He gives a little nod. "That's fine," he says, leaning forward to change the channel. "So. Game show or the news?"

"Not the news please," I say. He clicks the knob three times over. The game show host looks really old. The shy man puts his elbows on his knees and he starts to call out answers to the trivia questions. I close my eyes and listen to the noise of winning fill the room.

WHAT YOU LEFT IN
THE DITCH

Steven returned from the war without lips.

This is quite a shock, said his wife Mary who had spent the last six months knitting sweaters and avoiding a certain grocery store where a certain young man worked and looked at her in that certain way. I expected lips. Dead or alive, but with lips.

Steven went into the living room where his old favorite chair stood, neatly dusted and unused. I-can-eat-like-normal, he said in a strange halted clacking tone due to the plastic disc that covered and protected what was left of his mouth like the end of a pacifier. The-doctors-are-going-to-put-new-skin-on-in-a-few-weeks-anyway. Skin-from-my-palm. He lifted up his hand and looked at it. That-will-work, I-guess, he said. It-just-won't-be-quite-the-same.

No, said Mary, it won't. That bomb, she said, standing on the other side of the chair, you know it took the last real kiss from you forever, and as far as I can remember, that kiss was supposed to be mine.

That night in bed, he grazed the disc over her raised nipples like a UFO and the plastic was cool on her skin. It felt like they were in college and toying with desk items as sexual objects. Her boyfriend of that time, Hank: Let's try a ruler. Let's measure you, Mary. Let's balance a paperweight on my dick. I'm over that, Mary thought. I want lips now. I just want the basics.

She didn't say anything, but began to shop at the other grocery store again.

The young man there had always had lips but now they seemed twice as large and full and incredible, as if his face was overflowing with lip. While he ran her milk and eggs and toothpaste over the electronic sensor, she couldn't stop looking at them, guessing what they tasted like. The warm, salty taste of flesh.

Good to see you, he said, moving those lips. It's been a while.

Mary blushed and fiddled with the gum at the counter.

Just take a pack, he told her. I won't tell.

Really? She looked at the flavors and picked cinnamon.

Sure, he said, smiling at her, glancing around to see if his manager was in sight. Think of me while you chew.

She blushed again, pocketed the gum and then grabbed her two full bags in both arms.

Need help? he asked. Let me help you.

Okay. She passed the weight to him, and he walked her to the car which was parked near the river. While he placed the bags into the trunk, she was taken by the desire to join them. She wanted to sit in there and invite the man in with her, shut the trunk down and lock it and just make love and eat groceries until they suffocated or her husband needed the car.

Back at home, Steven was in the bathroom, looking at himself in the mirror. Mary stood and watched him touching the disc with his fingertips, a bag under each arm, until he felt her and turned around.

Honey, he said, back-so-soon! He took the bags from her, peered inside them and -oohed- and -aahed- over her food choices.

Oh-Mary, he said, God-I-missed-you-so-much. In-that-ditch, when-I-thought-of-you, I-saw-an-angel. His voice broke. I-saw-Mary, my-angel, in-this-house, with-these-bags. You-brought-me-back-home. He reached out his hand and fingers trickled down her arm.

She kept her back to him and shoved tin cans into the cupboard. Maybe, she was thinking, if you'd concentrated better you'd still have lips. Maybe you're not supposed to think of your wife at the market while people are throwing bombs at you. Maybe you're supposed to protect certain body parts so she'll be happy when you come back.

But instead she just piled the cans one on the other, edge to edge in tall buildings, kidney beans on top of tuna. She turned to Steven.

You're alive, she said, and hugged him. You're Steven. He pressed the disc hard to her cheek and kissed her, - - -, and she held herself in and tried not to shatter.

Steven ate more than she remembered so she was back at the market in two days. The young man was there, and she offered him a stick of the same cinnamon gum. He grinned at her.

Thanks, he said, taking a piece.

She touched the back of his hand while he was writing her driver's license number on the check, and said, Do you take care of yourself?

He looked up at her. What do you mean?

I mean, what if they called you to fight in the war? Her hand was stilled on his.

He snapped his gum. He drew a little gun on a corner of her check. No, he said, I don't think I would do it. I think I'd run away, because, you know, I don't want to fight in the war. I mean, how would you do it anyway? How would you know what to do? He drew little bullets coming out of the gun and sliding down the side of the check, near where her name and address were printed.

Mary nodded and placed her license back into her wallet.

I know, she said, me too. I would move away somewhere else. I wouldn't leave people and maybe never come back. You can't do that to people, you know?

Right, he said, looking up at her: I know what you mean. The most unbearable thing is losing someone like that.

Oh no, she said to him, wrapping the plastic handle of the

bag around her wrist several times, I don't think so. I don't agree. The most unbearable thing I think by far, she said, is hope.

At night Steven twitched with nightmares. He never used to; he used to sleep straight through the night, and Mary would carve shapes into his back with her stub of a fingernail and watch the goose bumps rise and fall like small mountain populations. Now he was bucking in and out of the sheets and she still carved the shapes and the goose bumps still emerged, but they didn't calm him. She wondered what he was seeing. Sometimes she woke him up.

Steven, she said, it's okay. You're here. You're back.

He looked up at her with a frame of sweat around his face and breathed out. -Mary-, he clacked, it's-Mary.

It's Mary, she said. Yes. That's me.

He held her so tightly she was uncomfortable. She wiggled loose and finally fell asleep for a couple of hours but woke up again in the middle of the night and left the bedroom. Steven was sleeping quietly, his back to her, arm out, palm open, belly sloping down to the sheets. She tried the TV but everything was either without plot or in the middle so she couldn't understand what was going on. Clicking it off, she went and sat in the backyard, on the edge of the patio with its red paint chipping. The sky was oddly light, but it was nowhere near morning.

Leaning down into the dirt, she began to dig a hole. The

dirt was grainy and soft and lifted out easily, and she wondered why she never took up gardening. It's supposed to be so soothing, she thought. Perhaps that is the soothing that I need.

She leaned down into the dirt and dug until there was a hole a few feet deep. She placed her feet in it.

I built this hole, she said, now what to put in it? She wandered in through the kitchen to the hall closet, opened it and saw the three sweaters she knit for Steven At War piled on the shelf by the sewing machine. There, she said, my sweaters. He won't want these. No one wears sweaters here anyway.

She lugged all three sweaters outside and gently folded them, placing them on top of each other in the hole. She remembered knitting them, singing songs into the thread about Steven, pretending she was keeping him alive although she knew he was dead. He had to be dead. She was just more honest with herself than the other wives. With each purl and knit and knot, she felt the coldness of his stiffening legs, the draining of color from his cheeks, knew that never would she feel his forearms warm and veined around her waist, never again would his voice whisper praise into her ear.

She let the dirt dribble through her fingers over the pile of sweaters and it slid down the sides, slowly filling up the space, covering the colorful sleeves. Dead sweaters, she thought. Isn't that funny, the way it turned out?

. . .

At the grocery store, the young man was wearing a gray button-up shirt and looked particularly handsome.

I was hoping you'd come in, he told her. I was thinking about you.

Really? His skin was so young, so new.

I get off in just a few minutes. He looked at his watch. Do you want to go on a walk or something? We're right by the river and I could use a break before I go home.

She watched the bag-packer put the eggs haphazardly on top.

Sure, she said. Why not.

She packed the bags in her trunk again and after a beat, pulled out the bouquet of gardenias that she'd bought because they'd smelled so strongly. She waited for the young man, feeling like a bride. After a minute, he exited the store without his apron, let loose, looking younger.

This way, he said, come this way. Nice flowers.

She felt embarrassed and asked him to hold them for her, which he did, blooms down. They walked side by side and she was aware of his breathing, easy and confident, and aware of his lips. Lips, she thought. I really really miss lips.

The river leapt over stones, gurgling as rivers do. Its voice lowered and deepened as they walked and the young man told her about his life, about how this was his summer job away from college and one day he wanted to own an art supply store. Interesting, she told him, that will be an interesting store to own. You will buy many different colors of paint.

Yeah, he said. I like paint.

The river was speeding up. It made a rushing noise, rocks breaking up the water into foam.

I want to throw myself in, she thought. I want to crack up on those rocks.

She looked at the young man.

Can you swim? she asked.

Oh, yeah, he said. I'm a great swimmer.

Would you rescue me, she said, if I went in? Because I'm not a good swimmer.

Went in that? He pointed to the river just in case there was a choice he didn't know about. It's cold in that, he said, and fast. Not a good idea to go in there if you can't swim.

But, like I said, she said, would you save me?

He seemed confused. This was not what he expected from her. I guess I'd try, he said, you know, if it was really dangerous. He took a step back. She walked to him.

I'm glad, she said.

He stepped down to a lower plain so he was suddenly her height and she went into his face and kissed those lips, reminded herself. They were so soft. She kissed him for a moment, and then she had to move away; they were too soft, the softness was murdering her.

Hey, said the young man, nice.

Mary sat down on the ground and felt like she could not possibly survive with something that soft in the world with her. The two of them could not exist together. No. The young man sat down, he wanted to kiss her again but she said, I have to go now. Did I tell you I was married?

No, he said, I didn't know you were married. He looked to her hand and pointed to the ring. Oh, right. Check it out. Cool.

She thought about Steven and the disc and about pressing her lips down on those plastic curves, pushing hard on them until she pressed her face into his. Pushed past his skin and through his bone and into the quiet warm space underneath, her eyes shut, cell to cell, both unarmed. In there, she thought, inside his mind and flooded with blood, without windows or doors or her knitting or his chair, maybe in there she could hold their faces in her hands and consider something like forgiveness.

She stood up and the young man reached out his unflowered hand, wanting to pull her to him, wanting her attention again.

Really, he said, I would rescue you, you know, what you were saying before.

Yeah, she said, I'm sure you'd try.

She started back along the path and he followed her. He was so young, he just talked about himself again and she tuned out and watched the shadows of the trees cut lines into the ground. She kicked a few rocks. Back in the parking lot, she held out her hand and grasped his for a second. He had a firm grip.

Come back, I'll give you more free gum, he said, handing her back her flowers.

Okay, she said, I can always use free gum.

He walked away, looking confused, not really sure what happened, if he was rejected or not. Mary threw the gardenias into the passenger seat, climbed into her car and drove home. She forgot the rest of the groceries and left them in the trunk. Later, when she went to get them, it was only the milk that had spoiled, releasing its warm dank odor on the air.

Instead she scooped up the flowers and went in to see Steven. He was in his chair, taking a nap. She stood above him and watched him twitch, his hands fluttering as if he'd been drugged. He was in her house: her husband, the love of her life. He was back. He made it. He left; he returned. She wanted to know him again, to enter the nightmare and be in there with him, to fight the demons with her own good weapons. She wanted to join him, but the chair was too small and his brain was his only and all she saw in the ditch were sweaters and a too light sky.

She reached out to shake him awake but her hand stopped in the air and wouldn't go farther. No hand was reaching out for her. Stirring in his sleep, he let out a clipped yell. Mary kneeled on the carpet.

Steven, she whispered, I miss you so, but everything is fine at home.

Steven, she said, the neighbors got a dog and I am growing out my hair.

She bowed her head. Removing the plastic wrap, she very carefully kissed the bouquet of gardenias and then placed it onto his stomach.

Here love, she said, I brought you some flowers.

She kept her head low. Steven stirred and eyes blinking, woke up to the smell of the gardenias.

-Mary-, he said, -flowers-, how-beautiful.

She put her hands over her ears and started to cry.

THE BOWL

Let me open it up for you.

There's a gift in your lap and it's beautifully wrapped and it's not your birthday. You feel wonderful, you feel like somebody knows you're alive, you feel fear because it could be a bomb, because you think you're that important.

When you open the wrapping (there's no card), you find a bowl, a green bowl with a white interior, a bowl for fruit or mixing. You're puzzled, but obediently put four bananas inside and then go back to whatever you were doing before: a crossword puzzle. You wonder and hope this is from a secret admirer but if so, you think, why a bowl? What are you to learn and gain from a green and white fruit bowl?

This is when you think about the last lover you had and feel bad about yourself. This is when you stand with your pencil poised over the crossword puzzle and stare at the wall. This is when you laugh out loud, alone, to yourself, at something funny he said once about crossword puzzles and feel ridiculous for still being able to be entertained by this lover of yore who slept facing the wall and wanted less than you wanted.

You want a lot.

You go to make yourself a cup of tea and while you're prepping your mug you spill the sugar all over the floor. It's sticky and gets all over your feet; this bothers you; you go to take a shower. As the shower water steams up the bathroom, it reminds you of the unfinished tea, and you dash naked into the kitchen to make sure you haven't left the burner on. The house a pile of ash with just the bathroom standing. You stand in front of the stove. The stove is off you say to it. You are off. You look at each burner in turn, then the oven part. All off. You go to take a shower and ignore your body. You use a soap puff brush instead of your hands, and when it's done, you're fresh and clean and disengaged and anybody.

At work: your boss has died. Really, you find out your boss has died of a heart attack, yesterday, in *his* shower, and your first thought is if you'll still have a job and your second thought is mean, like you wanted him to die anyway. He was a bad boss. At your desk, you feel guilty and not sure what to do; you have no boss, what are the rules? Who can you ask? You make a few lists of things to do and then sit still and do none of them. You think about the bowl and wonder if it has to do with your boss dying, was it some kind of message. You decide it is not a message, but mere coincidence.

At lunch you order steamed vegetables because you're re-

membering that you have a heart too. You feel humbled by
your heart, it works so hard. You want to thank it. You give
your chest a little pat. When the vegetables arrive, they are
twelve on the plate, high green and matte yellow, sliced into
fancy ovals and diamonds to disguise the fact that they taste so
bad. You pour lemon butter all over them but feel like a big
cheat. After several broccolis, you leave the restaurant with
your plate still half full and shiny with grease to go visit your
brother. He works in the fire department and is handsome in
his outfit. You tell him your boss is dead, and it freaks him
out. He wonders if he could've saved him, had he been there,
you know, he knows CPR. Your brother has your face, but a
better version, you look better as a man. You think about the
women who have loved him and looked into his face while
he entered their bodies, and how that's your face, almost, but
also definitely not. You feel gypped.

"Andy," you ask him, "will you set me up with a fireman?"

He laughs. "Sure." You've never asked this before, you
wonder if he thinks you're kidding.

You go home early because your boss is dead. The fruit
bowl sits there, some strange reminder of something you can't
remember. You put the bananas back on the counter and fill
the bowl with warm water. You let your hands soak in it, this
feels really nice. You sing a little song to yourself, about fruit
and bowls and warm water, a song you just made up. You
wonder if you'll go out with the fireman after all, and if you
do, will he kiss you? Does a fireman kiss slow or urgent? Will

he lift your shirt or run off to water things down just when it's all seeming better?

You lie down flat on the orange carpet and close your eyes. You are feeling very lonely. There is a knock at the door, and at first, you wonder if you made it up because you are so lonely. But then there's another knock, and this one is too emphatic to be part of a fantasy. This one is not a nice knock.

You look into the peephole. There's a man in a suit. You wonder if he's here to investigate if you killed your boss or not. You open the door.

"I'm here," he says, "to retrieve a bowl."

"What?" His eyebrows stick out from his face, adding great depth. He is an older man, he looks as though his life is not making him happy.

"I'm here to retrieve a fruit bowl. I think one of them was delivered to you this morning by accident. All wrapped up? A green fruit bowl?"

You are stunned and confused, it was not for you after all? You empty out the water, and hand him the fruit bowl and he nods. He drips the remaining drops of water onto your welcome mat. The man seems very displeased, and you think it's something you did, but then realize it has nothing to do with you which is depressing. He tilts his head down slightly in apology, and leaves with the bowl. You shut the door behind him. You want it back. You want the bowl back. You open the door to yell after him, sir, that's my bowl, it came to my house with my name on the wrapping, that's my bowl, sir, give me back my bowl. But he's gone. You go to the sidewalk to look down the street, but he's gone. All you can see are three kids on bicycles, circling their driveways, seven years old, turning tight circles in their driveways because they're too scared to go where there might be cars.

MARZIPAN

One week after his father died, my father woke up with a hole in his stomach. It wasn't a small hole, some kind of mild break in the skin, it was a hole the size of a soccer ball and it went all the way through. You could now see behind him like he was an enlarged peephole.

Sharon! is what I remember first. He called for my mother, sharp, he called her into the bedroom and my sister Hannah and I stood outside, worried. Was it divorce? We twisted nervously and I had one awful inner jump of glee because there was something about divorce that seemed a tiny bit exciting.

My mother came out, her face distant.

Go to school, she said.

What is it? I said. Hannah tried to peek through. What's wrong? she asked.

They told us at dinner and promised a demonstration after dessert. When all the plates were cleared away, my father raised his thin white undershirt and beneath it, where other people have a stomach, was a round hole. The skin had curved and healed around the circumference.

What's that? I asked.

He shook his head. I don't know, and he looked scared then.

Where is your stomach now? I asked.

He coughed a little.

Did you eat? Hannah said. We saw you eat.

His face paled.

Where did it go? I asked and there we were, his two daughters, me ten, she thirteen.

You have no more belly button, I said. You're all belly button, I said.

My mother stopped clearing the dishes and put her hand on her neck, cupping her jaw. Girls, she said, quiet down.

You could now thread my father on a bracelet. The giantess' charm bracelet with a new mini wiggling man, something to show the other giantesses at the giantess party. (My, my! they declare. He's so active!)

My parents went to the doctor the next day. The internist took an X ray and proclaimed my father's inner organs intact. They went to the gastroenterologist. He said my father was digesting food in an arc, it was looping down the sides, sliding around the hole, and all his intestines were, although further crunched, still there and still functioning.

They pronounced him in great health.

My parents walked down into the cool underground parking lot and packed into the car to go home.

Halfway there, ambling through a green light, my mother told my father to pull over which he did and she shoved open the passenger side door and threw up all over the curb.

They made a U-turn and drove back to the doctor's.

The internist took some blood, left, returned and winked.

Looks like you're pregnant, he said.

My mother, forty-three, put a hand on her stomach and stared.

My father, forty-six, put a hand on his stomach and it went straight through to his back.

They arrived home at six-fifteen that night; Hannah and I had been concerned—six o'clock marked the start of Worry Time. They announced the double news right away: Daddy's fine. Mommy's pregnant.

Are you going to have it? I asked. I like being the youngest, I said. I don't want another kid.

My mother rubbed the back of her neck. Sure, I'll have it, she said. It's a special opportunity and I love babies.

My father, on the couch, one hand curled up and resting inside his stomach like a birdhead, was in good spirits. We'll name it after my dad, he said.

If it's a girl? I asked.

Edwina, he said.

Hannah and I made gagging sounds and he sent us to our room for disrespecting Grandpa.

In nine months, my father's hole was exactly the same size and my mother sported the biggest belly around for miles. Even the doctor was impressed. Hugest I've ever seen, he told her.

My mother was mad. Makes me feel like shit, she said that night at dinner. She glared at my father. I mean, really. You're not even that tall.

My father growled. He was feeling very proud. Biggest belly ever. That was some good sperm.

We all went to the hospital on delivery day. Hannah wandered the hallway, chatting with the interns; I stood at my mother's shoulder, nervous. I thought about the fact that if my father lay, face down, on top of my mother, her belly would poke out his back. She could wear him like a huge fleshy toilet seat cover. He could spin on her stomach, a beige propeller.

She pushed and grimaced and pushed and grimaced. The doctor stood at her knees and his voice peaked with encouragement: Almost There, Atta Girl, Here We Go— And!

But the baby did not come out as planned.

When, finally, the head poked out between her legs, the doctor's face widened with shock. He stared. He stopped yelling Push, Push and his voice dried up. I went over to his side, to see what was going on. And what I saw was that the head appearing between my mother's thighs was not the head of a baby but rather that of an old woman.

My goodness, the doctor said.

My mother sat up.

I blinked.

What's wrong? said my father.

Hannah walked in. Did I miss anything? she asked.

The old woman kicked herself out the rest of the way, wiped a string of gook off her arm, and grabbing the doctor's surgical scissors, clipped the umbilical cord herself. She didn't cry. She said, clearly: Thank Heaven. It was so warm in there near the end, I thought I might faint.

Oh my God, said Hannah.

My mother stared at the familiar wrinkled face in front of her. Mother? she said in a tiny voice.

The woman turned at the sound. Sweetheart, she said, you did an excellent job.

Mother? My mother put a hand over her ear. What are you doing here? Mommy?

I kept blinking. The doctor was mute.

My mother turned to my father. Wait, she said. Wait. In Florida. Funeral. Wait. Didn't that happen?

The old woman didn't answer, but brushed a glob of blood off her wrist and shook it down to the floor.

My father found his voice. It's my fault, he said softly, and, hanging his head, he lifted his shirt. The doctor stared. My mother reached over and yanked it down.

It is not, she said. Pay attention to *me*.

Hannah strode forward, nudged the gaping doctor aside and tried to look up inside.

Where's the baby? she asked.

My mother put her arms around herself. I don't know, she said.

It's me, said my mother's mother.

Hi Grandma, I said.

Hannah started laughing.

The doctor cleared his throat. People, he said, this here is your baby.

My grandmother stretched out her wrinkled legs to the floor, and walked, tiny body old and sagging, over to the bathroom. She selected a white crepe hospital dress from the stack by the door. It stuck to her slippery hip. Shut your eyes, children, she said over her shoulder, you don't want to see an old lady naked.

The doctor exited, mumbling busy busy busy.

My mother looked at the floor.

I'm sorry, she said. Her eyes filled.

My father put his palm on her cheek. I grabbed Hannah and dragged her to the door.

We'll be outside, I said.

We heard her voice hardening as we exited. Nine months! she was saying. If I'd known it was going to be my *mother,* I would've at least smoked a couple of cigarettes.

In the hallway I stared at Hannah and she stared back at me. Edwina? I said and we both doubled over, cracking up so hard I had to run to the bathroom before I wet my pants.

. . .

We all drove home together that afternoon. Grandma in the backseat between me and Hannah wrapped up in the baby blanket she had knitted herself, years before.

I remember this one, she remarked, fingering its soft pink weave. I did a nice job.

My father, driving, poked his hole.

I thought it might be a baby without a stomach, he said to my mother in the front seat. I never thought this.

He put an arm on her shoulder.

I love your mother, he said, stroking her arm.

My mother stiffened. I do too, she said. So?

I hadn't gone to my father's father's funeral. It had been in Texas and I'd just finished with strep throat and everyone decided Hannah and I would be better off with the neighbors for the weekend. Think of us Sunday, my mother had said. I'd worn black overalls on Sunday, Hannah had rebelled and worn purple, and together we buried strands of our hair beneath the spindly roots of our neighbor's potted plants.

When they returned, I asked my father how it was. He looked away. Sad, he said, fast, scratching his neck.

Did you cry? I asked.

I cried, he said. I cry.

I nodded. I saw you cry once, I assured him. I remember, it was the national anthem.

He patted my arm. It was very sad, he said, loudly.

I'm right here, I told him, you don't have to yell it.

He went over to the wall and plucked off the black-and-white framed photograph of young Grandpa Edwin.

He sure was handsome, I said, and my father rested his hand on top of my head—the heaviest, best hat.

After we arrived home from the hospital, Hannah and I settled Grandma in the guest bedroom and our parents collapsed in the den: our father, bewildered, on the couch, our mother flat-backed on the floor, beginning a round of sit-ups.

Fuck if my mother is going to ruin my body, she muttered. Fuck that shit.

I brought a book on sand crabs into the living room and pretended to read on the couch. Hannah promptly got on the phone. No really! I heard her saying. I swear!

My father watched my mother: head, knees. Up, down.

At least you can *do* sit-ups, he said.

She sat-up, grit her teeth, and sat-down. Some good sperm, she said, nearly spitting.

It's miracle sperm, my father said.

Excuse me, I said, I'm in the room.

Miracle? my mother said. Make it your dad then. Tell your fucking chromosomes to re-create *him*.

Her breasts leaked, useless, onto her T-shirts—cloudy milk-stain eyes staring blind up at the ceiling. She did a set of a hundred and then lay flat.

Mommy, I said, are you okay?

I could hear Hannah in the other room: She died in October, she was saying. Yeah, I totally saw.

My mother turned her head to look at me. Come here, she said.

I put down my book, went over to her and knelt down.

She put a hand on my cheek. Honey, she said, when I die?

My eyes started to fill up, that fast.

Don't die, I said.

I'm not, she said, I'm very healthy. Not for a while. But when I do, she said, I want you to let me go.

I was able to attend my mother's mother's funeral. I kept close to Hannah for most of it, but when the majority of relatives had trickled out, I found my mother huddled into a corner of the white couch—her head back, face drawn.

I sat next to her, crawled under her arm and said, Mama, you are so sad.

She didn't move her head, just petted my hair with her hand and said: True, but honey, I am sad plus.

Plus what I never asked. It made me not hungry, the way she said it.

She stopped her sit-ups at ten-thirty that night. It was past my bedtime and I was all tucked in, lights out. Before she'd fallen asleep, Hannah and I had been giggling.

Maybe I'll have you, I said, stroking my stomach.

She'd sighed. Maybe I'll have myself, she'd whispered.

That concept had never even crossed my mind. Oldest, I hissed back.

After a while, she'd stopped answering my questions. I prodded my stomach, making sure it was still there and still its usual size. It growled back.

I heard my mother let out a huge exhale in the den and the steady count: three hundred and five, three hundred and six, stopped.

Stepping quietly out of bed, I tiptoed into the hallway; my father was asleep on the couch, and my mother was neatening up the bookshelves, sticking the horizontal books into vertical slats.

Mommy, I called.

She didn't turn around, just held out her arm and I went right to it.

My baby, she said, and I felt myself blooming.

We sat down on the couch, curled together, my knees in a V on her thigh. Her side was warmer than usual from the sit-ups, even a little bit damp. She leaned her head against mine and we both stared ahead, at the closed drapes that were ivory, specked with brown.

I'm hungry, I said.

Me too.

We stood and went to the refrigerator. I found some left-over spaghetti. My mother opened the freezer doors, rummaged around and brought out half a cake.

I never knew there was cake in there, I mumbled, stuffing a forkful of noodles into my mouth.

It was chocolate on the outside and sealed carefully in plastic.

This was from Grandma's funeral, she told me.

I blinked. No way, I said. The marzipan one? I *loved* that cake.

You tried it? My mother unwrapped it.

I ate at least three pieces, I said. It was the best food at the wake by far.

She cut me a thin slice and put it on my place mat.

Most ten-year-olds don't like marzipan, she told me. It's Grandma's favorite, marzipan is, she said. You must've gotten the taste from her.

I nibbled at its edge. It was cold and grainy from the freezer.

Delicious, I said, savoring the almond paste as it spread out in my mouth.

My mother cut herself a piece, grabbed a fork from the drying rack and sat down across from me.

Why do we have it? I asked.

She shrugged. You know some people keep pieces of wedding cake, she said, taking a bite.

In the morning, my father was holding the photograph of his father in his lap.

Edwin, I said. Handsome Grandpa Edwin.

He pulled me close to him. Grandpa Edwin had thick brown curls.

He really was an asshole, my father said.

I started laughing: loud, full laughter.

He put a hand over my mouth and I laughed into his palm. Sssh, Lisa, he said. Don't laugh about it.

It's funny, I mumbled.

Don't laugh at a dead man, he said.

I had a few left in me and I let them out, but they were half their big belly laugh size by then.

How's the hole? I asked, when I was done. Does it hurt?

Nah, he said. It's no big deal.

Can I see?

He raised his thin undershirt.

Can I touch? I asked. He nodded. I gingerly put my fingertips on the inner circle; his skin felt like skin.

So where do you think it went? I asked.

What, he said, the skin?

Everything, I said: the skin, the ribs that were in the way, the stomach acid, all of it.

I guess it's all still in there, he said. I guess it's just pushed to the side.

I think it's cool, I said, imagining a new sports game kind of like basketball that revolved around my father.

He put his shirt back down, a curtain falling. I don't, he said. But it didn't kill me, he said, and I'm grateful for that.

. . .

At dinner my grandmother cooked her famous soup with tiny hot dogs floating in a thick bean broth.

I missed this soup, I said, I never thought I'd eat this soup again. This is my favorite soup in the whole world.

Hannah promptly lost a piece of bread inside and poked around the bowl with her fork.

Let's hold hands, said my mother, before we start.

I swallowed the spoonful in my mouth.

I grabbed Hannah's hand and my grandmother's hand. One was soft and mushy and the other one was soft and mushy, but different kinds of soft and different kinds of mushy.

My mother closed her eyes.

We never say prayers, I interrupted.

We are today, said my mother.

I bowed my head.

So what do we say? I asked, looking down into my soup which was bobbing along. Something about bread?

Sshh, said my father. It's a silent prayer.

No, it's not that, said my mother, I'm still thinking.

Ow, Hannah told my father, you're squeezing too hard.

I think we're supposed to be thankful, I hinted.

Hannah turned and glared at me. Shut up, she said. Give her a second.

My grandmother was quiet, smelling her soup.

Needs salt, she whispered.

My mother looked up.

I'm not sure what to say, she said. Her eyebrows furrowed, uncertain.

Let's make it up, I said. I squeezed Hannah's hand and my grandma's hand, and at the same time, they squeezed back.

I'll start it, I said, and we'll go around the circle.

My mother looked relieved. Good, she said, that sounds good.

I would like to say thanks, I began, for my parents and my sister and for the special appearance of Grandma . . . I turned to Hannah.

. . . And for Grandma's soup which is the best soup and is way better than that fish thing we were going to eat. She faced my father.

He cleared his throat. There's usually something about survival in good prayers, he said. Thanks for that.

My mother gave him a look. That's so impersonal, she said.

He shrugged. I'm on the spot, he said. Survival is important to me.

My mother looked us all over and I could see the candle flame flickering near her eye. Her gaze held on her mother.

We all waited.

It's your turn, I said, in case she'd forgotten.

She didn't look at me. She stood up, breaking the handlinks she had made, and sat close to her mother.

My father began eating his soup.

I have a cake from your funeral, she said.

I felt myself lift inside. I squeezed down on Hannah's hand. She said Ouch.

Cake? my grandmother said. What kind of cake?

Marzipan cake, my mother said.

My grandmother smiled. Marzipan? she said. That's my favorite.

I stood up; I wanted to be the one; I went to the freezer, opened it, dug around and found the cake wedged beneath the third ice tray like a small football.

Here, I said. Here it is.

My mother grabbed it out of my hands.

Just a taste, she said.

Let's all have some! I said. We can all eat funeral cake!

Just a little, my mother said.

Oh come on! I said. Let's make it into five pieces.

My mother looked at me.

Okay, she said. Five pieces. Her face looked lined and tired as she cut up the cake. I passed a piece to each of us. My grandmother bit into hers right away.

Mmm, she said. That is good, now that is *good*.

My mother did not eat hers. She wrapped it back in the plastic.

My grandmother kept eating and oohing. I bit into mine. Hannah gave me hers; she hates marzipan. I nearly hugged her. My father ate his quickly, like an appetizer.

I remember, said my mother, we all thought you would've liked it. We said you would've loved it.

My grandmother licked her lips. I do love it, she said. She pointed. Are you going to eat your piece?

No, said my mother.

Can I have it? she asked. I haven't had such good marzipan in I don't know how long.

No, my mother said, closing her fingers over her piece. I want to keep mine, she said.

Oh come on, said my father, let the lady have her cake. It was her funeral cake for God's sake.

I finished my slice. I still had Hannah's.

Here, Grandma, I said, Hannah didn't want hers. I slid the whitish slab onto her plate.

Thank you dear, my grandmother said.

I want to keep mine, my mother repeated.

Hannah began on her soup. Her spoon made dull clinking sounds on the bowl.

The soup is good, Grandma, she said.

Mmm-hmm, said my father.

My mother sat still at her place. The plastic-wrapped cake sat next to her spoon. She didn't touch her soup. The hot dogs stopped floating and were still.

I'll eat yours if you don't want it, I said to my mother.

She pushed over her bowl. I pretended I was her while I ate it. I imagined I was doing the eating but she was getting nourished.

When I was done, I asked: May I be excused?

No one answered, so I stayed.

PART TWO

Quiet Please

Skinless

Fugue

Drunken Mimi

Fell This Girl

QUIET PLEASE

It is quiet in the rest of the library.

Inside the back room, the woman has crawled out from underneath the man. Now fuck me like a dog she tells him. She grips a pillow in her fists and he breathes behind her, hot air down her back which is starting to sweat and slip on his stomach. She doesn't want him to see her face because it is blowing up inside, red and furious, and she's grimacing at the pale white wall which is cool when she puts her hand on it to help her push back into him, get his dick to fill up her body until there's nothing left of her inside: just dick.

The woman is a librarian and today her father has died. She got a phone call from her weeping mother in the morning, threw up and then dressed for work. Sitting at her desk with her back very straight, she asks the young man very politely, the one who always comes into the library to check out bestsellers, asks him when it was he last got laid. He lets out a weird sound and she says shhh, this is a library. She has her hair back and the glasses on but everyone has a librarian fantasy, and she is truly a babe beneath.

I have a fantasy, he says, of a librarian.

She smiles at him but asks her original question again. She doesn't want someone brand new to the business but neither is she looking for a goddamn gigolo. This is an important fuck for her. He tells her it's been a few months and looks sheepish but honest and then hopeful. She says great and tells him there's a back room with a couch for people who get dizzy or sick in the library (which happens surprisingly often), and could he meet her there in five minutes? He nods, he's already telling his friends about this in a monologue in his head. He has green eyes and no wrinkles yet.

They meet in the back and she pulls the shade down on the little window. This is the sex that she wishes would split her open and murder her because she can't deal with a dead father; she's wished him dead so many times that now it's hard to tell the difference between fantasy and reality. Is it true? He's really gone? She didn't really want him to die, that is not what she meant when she faced him and imagined knives sticking into his body. This is not what she meant, for him to actually die. She wonders if she invented the phone call, but she remembers the way her mother's voice kept climbing up and up, and it's so real and true she can't bear it and wants to go fuck someone else. The man is tired now but grinning like he can't believe it. He's figuring when he can be there next, but she's sure she'll never want him again. Her hair is down and glasses off and clothes on the floor and she's the fucked librarian and he's looking at her with this look of adoration. She squeezes his wrist and then concentrates on putting herself back together. In ten minutes, she's at the front desk again, telling a youngster about a swell book on aisle ten, and unless you leaned forward to smell her, you'd never know.

There is a mural on the curved ceiling of the library of fairies dancing. Their arms are interwoven, hair loose from the wind. Since people look at the ceiling fairly often when they're at the library, it is a well-known mural. The librarian tilts her head back to take a deep breath. One of the fairies is missing a mouth. It has burned off from the glare of the sunlight, and she is staring at her fairy friends with a purple-eyed look of muteness. The librarian does not like to see this, and looks down to survey the population of her library instead.

She is amazed as she glances around to see how many attractive men there are that day. They are everywhere: leaning over the wood tables, straight-backed in the aisles, men flipping pages with nice hands. The librarian, on this day, the day of her father's death, is overwhelmed by an appetite she has never felt before and she waits for another one of them to approach her desk.

It takes five minutes.

This one is a businessman with a vest. He is asking her about a book on fishing when she propositions him. His face lights up, the young boy comes clean and clear through his eyes, that librarian he knew when he was seven. She had round calves and a low voice.

She has him back in the room; he makes one tentative step forward and then he's on her like Wall Street rain, his suit in a pile on the floor in a full bucket, her dress unbuttoned down, down, one by one until she's naked and the sweat is pooling in her back again. She obliterates herself and then buttons up. This man too wants to see her again, he might want to marry her, he's thinking, but she smiles without teeth and says, man, this is a one-shot deal. Thanks.

If she wanted to, she could do this forever, charge a lot of money and become rich. She has this wonderful body, with full heavy breasts and a curve to her back that makes her pliable like a toy. She wraps her legs around man number three, a long-haired artist type, and her hair shakes loose and he removes her glasses and she fucks him until he's shuddering and trying to moan, but she just keeps saying Sshhh, shhh and it's making him so happy, she keeps saying it even after he's shut up.

The morning goes by like normal except she fucks three more men, sending them out periodically to check her desk, and it's all in the silence, while people shuffle across the wood floor and trade words on paper for more words on paper.

After lunch, the muscleman enters the library.

He is tan and attractive and his arms are busting out of his shirt like balloons. He is with the traveling circus where he lifts a desk with a chair with a person with a child with a dog with a bone. He lifts it up and never drops anything and people cheer.

He also likes to read.

He picks this library because it's the closest to the big top. It's been a tiring week at the circus because the lion tamer had a fit and quit, and so the lions keep roaring. They miss him, and no one else will pet them because they're lions. When the muscleman enters the library, he breathes in the quiet in relief. He notices the librarian right away, the way she is sitting at her desk with this little twist to her lips that only a very careful observer would notice. He approaches her, and she looks at him in surprise. The librarian at this point assumes everyone in the library knows what is going on, but the fact is, they don't. Most of the library people just think it's stuffier than usual and for some reason are having a hard time focusing on their books.

The librarian looks at the muscleman and wants him.

Five minutes, she says, tilting her head toward the back room.

The muscleman nods, but he doesn't know what she's talking about. He goes off to look at the classics, but after five minutes, follows his summons, curious.

The back room has a couch and beige walls. When he enters the room, he's struck by the thickness of the sex smell; it is so pervasive he almost falls over. The librarian is sitting on the couch in her dress which is gray and covers her whole body. Down the center, there is a row of mother-of-pearl buttons and one of them is unbuttoned by accident.

The thing is, the muscleman is not so sure of his librarian fantasies. He is more sure that he likes to lift whatever he can. So he walks over to her in the waddly way that men with big thighs have to walk, and picks her up, couch and all.

Hey, she says, put me down.

The muscleman loves how his shoulders feel, the weight of something important, a life, on his back.

Hey, she says again, this is a library, put me down.

He twirls her gently, to the absent audience and she ducks her head down so as not to collide with the light fixture.

He opens the door and walks out with the couch. He is thoughtful enough to bring it down when they get to the door frame so she doesn't bump her head. She wants to yell at him but they're in the library now.

Two of the men she has fucked are still there, in hopes for a second round. They are stunned and for some reason very jealous when they see her riding the couch like a float at a parade, through the aisles of books. The businessman in the vest holds up a book and after a moment, throws it at her.

You are not Cleopatra! he says, and she ducks and screams, then clamps her hand over her mouth. Her father's funeral is in one day. It is important that there is quiet in a library. The book flies over her head and hits a regular library man who is reading a magazine at a table.

He throws it back, enraged, and they're all over in a second, pages raining down, the dust slapping up into her face. They rustle as they fly and the librarian covers her face because she can't stand to look down at the floor where the books are splayed open on their bindings as if they've been shot.

The muscleman doesn't seem to notice, even though the books are hitting him on his legs, his waist. He lifts her up, on his tiptoes, to the ceiling of the library.

Stand up, he says to her in a low voice, muffled from underneath the couch, stand up and I'll still balance you, I can do it even if you are standing.

She doesn't know what else to do and she can feel his push upward from beneath her. She presses down with her feet to stand, and puts a finger on the huge mural on the ceiling, the mural of the fairies dancing in summer. Right away, she sees the one fairy without the mouth again, and reaches into her bun to remove the pencil that is always kept there. Hair tumbles down. On her tiptoes, she is able to touch the curve of the ceiling where the fairy's mouth should be.

Hold still, she whispers to the muscleman who doesn't hear her, is in his own bliss of strength.

She grips the pencil and with one hand flat on the ceiling steadies herself enough to draw a mouth underneath the nose of the fairy. She tries to draw it as a big wide dancing smile, and darkens the pencil lining a few times. From where she stands, it looks nice, from where she is just inches underneath the painting which is warmed by the sunlight coming into the library.

She doesn't notice until the next day, when she comes to

work to clean up the books an hour before her father is put into the ground, that the circle of fairies is altered now. That the laughing ones now pull along one fairy with purple eyes, who is clearly dancing against her will, dragged along with the circle, her mouth wide open and screaming.

SKINLESS

Renny's phone privileges were revoked when they discovered a swastika carved into his bed board. He had been at Ocean House for three days. The staff, arguing in the Off-Limits Room with their hands warmed by white Styrofoam coffee cups, took an hour before they decided on this as a punishment. Jill Cohen, the activities director, went into his room while Renny was playing pool with Damon, the one who'd stabbed himself in the thigh, and turned the swastika into four boxes and then put a roof and a chimney on top. She wanted to make smoke coming out of the chimney, but the fork did not carve curls well, so she left the hearth cold.

Jill drove forty-five minutes every other day to run the evening activities for the group of runaway teenagers living at Ocean House. This was her first job out of college, and she had been thrilled when they accepted her. "The kids are supposed to be really troubled but really great," she'd told her college roommate, who was silently walking out the door with a banana box filled with books in her arms. "Good luck," they had said to each other, and then college was over. Jill had a new boyfriend named Matthew who liked to eat foods so spicy they made him cough. His body was covered with fair, shining hair, and in bed, with the side lamp on, he seemed to almost glow. When he held her while they made love, she would sometimes imagine scratching off his skin, scratching repeatedly with her nails until the layers peeled off and she discovered that beneath that sheath of flesh, he was made entirely out of pearl.

How? she'd splutter, and he'd laugh and kiss light into her mouth.

She often remembered the day she first grew breasts, how her usually olive skin was covered with red, crisscrossing stretch marks, like a newly revealed secret map to the treasures of her body.

Renny ran away from home because his older brother Jordan came to visit. Returning home from a friend's house one afternoon, Renny found Jordan's green truck parked crooked, taking over the driveway. Renny kept going as if he didn't even recognize the house. As he walked, he gathered a globule of spit in his mouth in case he saw anyone who looked, in any way, dark. He walked straight, over an hour, to the sagging framework of Ocean House because you only had to stay for a couple weeks, the food was supposed to be decent, and if you were lucky, he'd heard you might even meet other members of the Resistance there.

Jill hung up the phone with her mother, and looked searchingly at Matthew. He was sitting on the sofa, balancing the remote control on his knee. "You know," she said, "that if we had kids, they'd be rightfully Jewish. You know that, right?"

He nodded. His eyes were on the TV.

"I think it would be okay with me, as long as you don't think it's totally important to teach them all about Christ, do you? You don't believe in Christ, do you?"

"Not really, but Jill, we're not getting married."

"I know," she said, pulling on her earlobe, "but just in case?"

"Jill," he said, "we're not getting married."

But she couldn't get the wedding out of her head. There would be both a rabbi and a priest, and the priest would have no hairs on the backs of his hands, like a young boy. She walked over to Matthew, eyebrows pulling down. "If you know that for sure," she said, "then why are we going out?"

Matthew drew her onto his lap. "How long till you have to leave for work?"

"Half hour," she said, absently rubbing the top of his wrist. "Just in case," she said, "it's mainly a cultural thing."

"Half an hour is plenty of time," he said and he reached his hand up her shirt. "Shhh, Jill, sshh."

Renny's father was dead, but his brother was eight years older, in the army, and handsome. He wrote home once a month, one side of one page, from a country with unusual stamps. Jordan was well loved by women, and had three illegitimate children spread over the country. He never called them, met them, touched them.

At thirteen, Renny captured his brother's little black phone book in an effort to find information on these mothers. He carefully copied their names and numbers onto the inside of his closet door.

"Little shit," Jordan said to Renny when he found him frozen in the closet, phone book in lap, "what are you doing with my book?"

Renny leaned his back carefully against the door, hiding his writing. "Just looking at all the people you know," he said, half-holding his breath.

"Impressed?" Jordan asked, looking down and smiling.

"Oh yeah," Renny said, "lots of girls."

Jordan pulled his brother up and put one big hand on Renny's neck. "Just don't fuck with my stuff, little brother, okay? You ask first." He tightened his grip, then let go. "Nosy fuck."

Renny sank back to the floor. Jordan went into the backyard to smoke a cigarette. Renny waited until he heard the screen door slam, and then turned around to look at the numbers. They were smudged, but still readable. He leaned his forehead on the wood of the door frame and breathed in the bitter smell of the lacquer.

Jill's mother, in phase three of her career, was the owner of a Jewish dating service. She tried to meet at least three new Jews a day and convince them that she held their ticket to marital bliss. Often, she did. Her agency had something like a 75 percent success rate because it only accepted customers who were willing to work and commit, and who had abandoned their Prince Charming/Virgin-Whore fantasies. Jill worked there during summers and had met every available Jewish man in Los Angeles. She dated some, liked some, but was required by the agency to fill out a date report after each encounter. Her mother liked to supplement her daughter's questionnaire with new, handwritten inquiries, like: What do you appreciate in a good kiss, Jill? At first she answered these questions openly, believing it was part of that mother/daughter "we are now best friends" syndrome. But suddenly, her dates began to execute these perfect kisses, and the third time a man tipped up her chin gently before he laid his lips on hers, Jill ran, yelling, to her mother and quit the job. Her mother did not understand. But Jill remembered that the woman was, in fact, not her best friend but her mother, and proceeded to divulge the kissing facts only to her friends, telling her mother instead about her intricate opinions on all the recently released movies.

On Saturdays, when rates were lower, Renny called Boston, Atlanta and Hagerstown, Maryland. Often, the mothers were home taking care of their new babies, usually crying in the background.

"Hello, Mrs. Stevens," he said in his best older voice, "I'm calling from *Parents* magazine, may I have a few minutes of your time?" If they said no, he plowed ahead anyway. "Is your baby happy? How old is your baby? Would you describe your baby as a fun-loving baby or a serious baby? Does your baby more resemble you or the father?" Sometimes he slipped up and asked questions too personal, and the women began to fall suspect, and hang up. He called them, on average, every two months. Sometimes he was a contest man, asking them to send photos to a P.O. box and enter My Baby's the Cutest! contest. Maybe they would win $100,000! Sometimes he just pretended he'd gotten the wrong number. He liked to hear their voices. They sounded tired, but kind.

"We're drawing our dreams tonight," Jill announced to the group of seven teenagers in front of her.

"You must've been such a geek in high school," Trina said.

"No hostile comments," Jill said, smoothing down her red

Gap T-shirt. "If you're mad about something, maybe you should tell the group."

"I don't think any of us want to be here for that long," Trina said. She smiled at Damon. "And it still wouldn't change you being a geek in high school."

Jill passed out pencils and papers. "I was not a geek," she said. "Do you want to do this or not?"

"Go ahead, Jill," said Damon, smiling. "Dreams. Cool. Trina's a geek too, she just doesn't want you to know."

"Oh, shut up, Damon." Trina rolled her foot into his lap. No sex was allowed at Ocean House, guests would be expelled. Damon circled her ankle quickly and gave it a squeeze. Trina pulled it out, and relaxed.

"Any crayons?" George asked. No one liked him. He smiled too much and made jokes about cyberspace that were either stupid or confusing. Jill pulled a 64 crayon box out of her huge, denim purse.

Renny watched her carefully rezip her purse. Then he leaned back and drew circles on his paper. He put the eraser end of his pencil in his stomach and pushed it in until it ached. He imagined Jill, emaciated and naked, her hair in strings, trying to speak to him in German, begging him for mercy.

"Did my drawing, Jilly," he said.

She looked it over. "You dream about bubbles?"

"Ha ha." He looked at the other residents who were, mostly, doodling. Damon was drawing a big eye.

Renny leaned over. "Eyes the color of sky . . . ?" he

asked. He hadn't pegged Damon for the Resistance because he talked to Trina, the black girl, so much, but you never knew.

"You a poet?" Damon said, turning around to face Renny. "I never knew we had such a wonderful poet among us." Renny leaned back. No one here but him. He filled in the circles with black crayon.

"I dream about the insides of olives," he told Jill. "I dream about big black holes."

One mother sent a photograph to Renny's P.O. box. The baby was a girl, half black, dark, dark eyes and a serious face. Her arms reached toward the camera, wanting to play with the lens. "Nicole Shaw," it read on the back, "ten months old." Renny took the picture to the park with him and stared at his niece for an hour. He could feel her, how heavy she would be in his arms, how she would fall asleep and curl her head into his chest, enamored by the unfamiliar arms of a boy. Are you my daddy? she would ask. He looked into her eyes, and he could see in them, already, already, that death of loneliness, covering her like a thin gauze, impossible to remove. He picked up a twig and scraped at her face. The colors eased off, thin white stripes crossing through her tiny body. He erased Nicole and her arms and her eyes until she was just scratches on a piece of film.

· · ·

Matthew broke up with Jill because she wouldn't go on the pill. She said she'd go on the pill only if he would move in with her, and he looked at her like she was crazy, and said he hated condoms, they had to have a change. I get bladder infections, she told him, I can't use a diaphragm. Let's wait a little while, and maybe I will go on the pill, if it seems like we're more serious. I'm not serious, he told her, I don't want a real relationship now. Maybe you do, but you're scared, she said. Maybe I'm not, he said back. I think we want different things. I have to go to work, she said. In a half hour. Go early, he said, maybe there's traffic.

"We're going to do trust exercises today," Jill stated.

"Fabulous," said Trina, glaring at Damon.

Jill cleared her throat and continued. "One of you is blind-folded, and the other leads the first person around the house and the backyard, being gentle and trustworthy, and then you switch. It's scary because you're used to using your eyes so much, but it's a nice way to learn about trusting each other. Okay, pick partners."

Trina and Damon were an obvious pair. The two cocaine addicts who giggled a lot and were pretty nice to Renny grabbed hands. George, the outcast, looked toward Renny who looked away, realizing there was an odd number; George was paired with Lana, the very quiet, beautiful one who moved in slow motion like she was underwater and never told anyone why she was there.

"Did your math wrong, Jilly," Renny said, kicking out his boots and running his palm over the smooth splinters of hair poking out of his skull.

"No, you'll be my partner, Renny," Jill said. He blanched.

"I don't want to do it," he said.

"It's tonight's activity," Jill said. Her eyes were tired from crying about Matthew. "Do you want to go first, or shall I?"

"You go. Get blindfolded," Renny said. She selected a blue bandanna from the stack. "Do you trust me, Jilly?" he asked.

"Yes," she said, tying the cloth at the back of her head and letting the triangles fall over most of her face. She stood directly in the middle of the room, arms straight down her sides. "Please don't call me Jilly, Renny. Lead me around. I trust you."

Her mother had taken her to lunch that day. Jill hadn't wanted to mention the breakup with Matthew.

"I forget, honey, is he cute?" her mother asked, bright eyes boring into her daughter. Jill had never brought Matthew home to be scrutinized.

"He's not blond," Jill said, "if that's what you mean."

"I don't know what you mean," her mother said, "I'm sure he's a very nice boy. His parents come from where, again?"

"I don't know." Jill wished she could lay her cheek down

on her plate and just rest there with the cold porcelain. "Whatever. It's not serious." Her voice was fading.

"But do you want it to be?" Mrs. Cohen asked, a piece of French bread stilled in her hand.

"Doesn't really matter, does it, whether or not I want it to be. It's not."

"Well, it could always become serious, right?" She scooped up some white butter with her knife and spread it on the bread. "Does he talk about commitment?"

"We broke up yesterday, Mother," Jill said finally. "It's not an issue. We're broken up. Stop asking questions."

Jill's mother took a bite out of the bread and chewed for a moment. "Well, I'm sorry to hear that," she said, and smiled.

After he got the photo in the P.O. box, Renny painted the inside of his closet door with white paint. He painted slowly up, then down, until the numbers had vanished, and the paint would never flake away. He went into the bathroom and tried to throw up, but he couldn't. Grabbing the leftover paint, he walked down to the train station. There was an empty cave where his older brother used to fuck girls, or smoke pot, or whatever he did before he left for the army. Renny painted seventeen swastikas, one for each year of his life, all over the cave and then curled up underneath them and went to sleep. The swastikas looked like spider boomerangs that he could fling out into the world. They would clear a path, and then come back, to guide him to safety.

. . .

Renny led Jill through the kitchen.

"Counter's on your left, fridge on your right," he said.

"Thanks." She walked up the stairs and down the stairs and through the back door into the yard.

"So do you like it here, Renny?" she asked.

"Yeah, it's okay," he said. "Step up. Just walk straight here." They reached the cliffs overlooking the beach, across the street from Ocean House. He could see the distant figures of the other residents, their tentative arms. He heard Trina laugh.

"Are we going too far?" Jill asked.

"We'll switch soon."

He stopped her at the edge of a cliff. The ground beneath them crumbled down for thirty feet, and then led into the sand, and then the water.

"We're at the edge of a cliff, Jill," Renny said, standing behind her, his hands cupping her shoulders.

"I'm trying to trust you here, Renny," she said. The wind blew her T-shirt to her skin. She watched the strange colors underneath her blindfold, and pictured Matthew's back growing smaller and smaller and how the world seemed to close in on her then.

"I hated what you did to my swastika," Renny said.

"Well I couldn't just leave it there," she said back. The palms of his hands were on her upper arms, warm. "I hate swastikas."

"See, Jill," Renny said, "it's eyes the color of sky, not of earth, that's what it's about, see, that's what we say. Eyes the color of sky, not of earth." He stared at her hair; it was dark and long and felt soft where it touched his hands.

"But Renny," she said, "your eyes are brown."

He gripped her shoulders. He wondered if by the time the two weeks were up, and he returned home, Jordan would be gone.

Jill pictured the wedding again. Except now the priest was nowhere to be found, the groom was nowhere to be found, and it was just herself and the rabbi. His arm was tan and thick with black hair. See our skin, the rabbi was telling her, this skin was made for the desert.

"It's a long way down," Renny said.

She imagined scratching at the skin on the rabbi's arm, scratching at her own arm, scratching them down, until underneath the thin layers of flesh she found out just what exactly they were made of.

"Are you scared?" Renny held her shoulders tightly.

"Should I be?"

Renny didn't answer. Jill shivered.

"Are you cold?" he asked.

"Yeah," she said, "a little."

He put his arms around her chest, and brought her closer to him. One thumb very gently brushed against the side of her nipple, standing up from the chill. She was quiet.

"Is that okay?" he asked.

"Yeah," she said. She breathed out, and closed her eyes

beneath the blindfold. Her skin was rising. I am made out of dirt, she thought.

"Do you want to switch?" Renny asked quietly. His hand was light against her breast.

I am made out of gold.

"No," she said, "do you?"

"No." He hugged her in closer and listened to the water rush at them from far away.

FUGUE

1. Dinnertime

I sit across the table from my husband. It is dinnertime. I made steak and green beans and homestyle potatoes and even clipped two red roses from the bush in the backyard; they stand in a vase between us which is clear so I can watch the stems drift in the water as he speaks.

He puts his elbows on the table. He opens his mouth while he chews. He gesticulates with his fork, prongs out.

Me, I nod and nod. He tells me all about work. The memos are misspelled, he tells me. That new secretary can barely speak. I listen and chew with my mouth closed. The potato, no longer hot, breaks under my teeth, melts across my tongue, my upper lip seals to my bottom lip, and everything is private inside my mouth—loud and powerful and mine. A whole world of noise going on in there that he can't even

79

hear. Reaching forward, he spears a big piece of potato with his fork. He lifts it up, takes it in, bites down. I watch the food disappearing in his mouth and it's my food and I bought it and I made it and I have to will my hands to keep still because I think I want to rescue it. I want to rescue my food, thrust an arm across the tablecloth, spill the drifting roses, dodge his molars, avoid his tongue, and seize it back, bring it all out, drag it down into the dish, until there is just a mush of alive potato between us, his stomach empty, my mouth still closed.

2.

Inside the pill factory, the muttering worker was switching things around.

"I'll put the yellow pills in here," he said to himself, mutter mutter, "and the white ones in here." He took the bottles to the child-sealing machine and went home.

Two weeks later, outside in the world, people with prescriptions fell down dead. The muttering worker read about it in the paper, felt a surge of importance, and decided it was time to move on. He called the pill factory office and told them he quit. They asked why. He said allergies. They said: Allergies to what? And he said, Allergies to the telephone and hung up.

This was the fourth job he'd grown tired of in a month. Two weeks before he'd gotten a gig teaching English to immigrants. He'd taught them the wrong things. He'd said:

pussy means woman and asshole means friend. During the week, one female student got propositioned. Two men were beaten up. They stomped into their classroom, bruised and confused, but their misleading muttering teacher was long gone—already shaking the hand of the pill factory boss, in fact, his eyes flicking with interest on the vats of colored ovals and the power hidden beneath their shells.

But now it was time to change again. The muttering man put on a tie and looked at himself in the mirror. This always made him spit. He projected it out, pleh, littering his face. The muttering man had been an ugly child. He had been an ugly teenager. Now he was an ugly adult. He found this pattern very annoying.

This time, he applied for a secretarial job. Decided he needed to do something calm and quiet for a while, like memos. Here he met his match: loud man.

Loud man wore a necklace, talked very loud and was very honest. He looked everyone square in the eye and said, Let me tell you what I honestly think and then did just that.

Muttering man hated him for several reasons, one being that loud man was his boss, another being that loud man was loud and the third and final and most awful being that loud man was good-looking. *Really* good-looking.

Muttering man went to loud man's house with a gun.

"Hello," he muttered, "I'm here to steal from you."

Loud man didn't quite hear him right. "You're here to what? Speak up."

"Steal," said muttering man as loud as he could which was

not loud at all, "I want to steal things. Like some jewelry. Like your mirror. Like your wife."

Loud man was angry, flushed a becoming pink and said many things, including Let me tell you what I honestly think.

"Please," muttered muttering man, "tell away."

"I think you're my employee!" said loud man in a huge voice, "and I Think You're Fired!"

Muttering man fired the gun and hit loud man in the knee. Loud man yelled and sat on the floor. Muttering man squared his shoulders and took what he asked for.

First, he told the trembling wife to wait at the door. He tried to catch a glimpse of her face, to see what kind of woman such a good-looking fellow would nab, but he couldn't see much underneath her overhanging hair.

Next, he told loud man to remove his gold necklace which he happily slipped over his own ugly head.

"I've never had a necklace," he muttered, pleased.

Finally, he walked up and down the halls looking for the perfect mirror to snatch. He passed several boring oval ones but when he turned the corner and walked into the master bedroom, he found exactly what he was looking for. Hanging on the wall, just opposite the large bed, was a huge rectangular mirror in a lavish silver frame. Mumbling under his breath in delight, muttering man gently lifted it off its hook. This mirror had been reflecting loud good-looking man for years and so had turned soft and complacent, and was likely to be kind to even muttering man's harsh features. He took a quick peek at his necklaced self and fought down the blast of hope.

With some difficulty, he angled the huge mirror under his arm and shoved the wife into the passenger seat of the car, leaving loud man howling in the house. Muttering man started the engine and took off down the street. He glanced sideways at the wife, examining her profile, searching for beauty. She was okay-looking. She didn't look like a movie star or anything. She looked sort of like four different people he'd met before. She stared straight ahead. After fifteen minutes, he dumped her off at the side of the road because she didn't talk and muttering man wasn't good with silent people. Plus, he wanted to be alone with the mirror.

"Bye," he said to her, "sorry."

She watched him through the window with large eyes. "That necklace is giving you a rash," she said. "It's made of nickel."

He itched the back of his neck. Before he pulled away, he threw her a couple cigarettes and a pack of matches from the glove compartment. She gave a little wave. Muttering man ignored her and pushed down on the gas. Less than ten miles later, he slowed and pulled to the side of the road. He lifted the mirror onto his lap. Running his fingers in and over the silvery nubs, he fully explored the outside before he dared to look in. He could sense the blob of his face sitting inside the frame, unfocused and patient, waiting to be seen.

3. Visitor at Haggie and Mona's

"Mona," said Haggie, "I'm tired."

Mona was stretching her leg up to the edge of the living room couch. "You're always tired," she said. She put her chin on her knee.

Haggie settled deeper into the green chair, the softest chair ever made. "Hand me that pillow, will you?"

"No." She reached forward and held her foot.

Haggie sighed. He could feel the start of that warm feeling inside his mouth, the feeling that he could catch sleep if he was quiet enough. He felt hyperaware of his tongue, how awkwardly it fit.

Leaning down, Mona spoke to her knee. "You'll just doze off and you sleep way too much," she said. "You practically just woke up."

"I know," he said, dragging a hand down his face, "you're absolutely right. Now hand me that pillow so I can take a nap and think about that."

"Haggie," said Mona, switching legs, "come on."

Mona was Haggie's one remaining friend. The rest had gone to other cities and lost his phone number. Haggie sat around all day, living off money in the bank from a car crash court settlement, while Mona trotted off each morning to work for a temp company. She typed something like a million words per minute. She was *always* offered the job at the place she temped, but she always said no. She liked the wanting far more than the getting, and, of course, was the same with men. She had this little box in her room containing already two disengaged engagement rings. She'd told the men: Sorry, I can't keep this, but oddly enough, they each had wanted her to. She seemed to attract very generous men. As a memento of me, they said, little knowing there was another such souvenir residing in a box on her dresser.

Haggie tugged on his tongue. It felt mushy and grainy and when he pinched it hard, he felt nothing.

"Are you doing anything tonight?" she asked, chin on her other knee.

"Me?" he garbled, still holding onto his tongue, "tonight?" Mona swung her leg down, and gripping the side of the couch like a barre, began a set of pliés.

He released his fingers and swallowed. "Tonight?" he said, clearly this time, "nothing. Those bowling friends of yours are having a party but I said no. They asked if you wanted to go but I said you didn't. Do you?" He paused. Mona didn't answer. "They all want you, you know."

"Really?" Mona, in mid-plié, dimpled up, pleased. "Which ones? All? Really? What exactly did they say?"

Haggie scratched his head. He didn't even know if it was true, he just liked to see Mona leap for things.

Mona bent down and touched her head to her knees. "I have a date anyway," she said, voice muted.

Haggie let his body slump into the chair. He hated it when Mona went out—the house felt dead without her. "Hey," he said, "please. The pillow?" He pointed again to the couch, just a few feet out of his reach. His blood felt weighted, each corpuscle dragging its own tiny wheelbarrow of rocks.

"Haggie." Mona shook out her legs and looked at him. "Go outside."

"Blech," he said to the ceiling, "I hate outside."

She walked over and stroked his hair. "Do something good," she said, "Haggie. Do something."

He leaned briefly into her hand. She smelled like vanilla and laundry detergent. "I really would," Haggie said, "you know, really. If I could only get out of this damn chair."

Mona touched his cheek. She stood next to him for a moment, then gave a little sigh and disappeared into her bedroom. Haggie turned his head and watched her doorway for a while, eventually closing his eyes. After forty-five minutes, Mona emerged, shiny, in a brown dress. Haggie was drifting off.

"Hag," she said. "Wait, wake up, I have a question." She twirled around. "High heels or not?" Haggie shook his head awake, looked at her and tried to focus.

"No," he said after a minute, voice gravelly, rubbing an eye, "you're too peppy already. Wear boots," he said. "Weigh yourself down a little."

She stuck out her tongue at him but vanished into her bedroom again and came out in two minutes wearing lace-up brown boots.

"Lovely," Haggie said.

There was a knock at the door.

"There he is," said Haggie, "Monsieur Pronto."

Mona looked at her watch. "No," she said, "I'm picking him up. Are you expecting anyone?"

He laughed. "My illicit lover," he said. He sank deeper into the chair. "Maybe we're getting mugged. Didn't I tell you? We should get bars on our windows."

The knock interrupted again: rap rap rap.

Mona went to the door. She peeped in the peephole. "It's a woman. Who is it?" she called.

A muffled voice came through.

Mona looked at Haggie. "Should I let her in?"

"Is she cute?" he asked.

Mona rolled her eyes. "I don't know," she said, "her hair is covering her face." She opened the door.

"Hello," said Mona, "how can I help you?"

The woman tugged off her wedding ring. "Please," she said, holding it forward, "please, will you take this in exchange for a place to stay?"

Haggie burst out laughing.

Mona shook her head. "Oh no," she said, "I can't keep that." The woman's hand was trembling as she held the ring forward, and the edge of her dress was charred black.

"Haggie," Mona said, "shut up. Stop laughing. She wants to stay here."

"Fine," he called from the chair, eyes closing. "But tell this one to keep the ring."

Mona opened the door wider. "Please," she said, "come on in, you look so tired." She took the woman by the elbow and guided her into the living room. "Haggie," she said, "get out of the chair, Hag, can't you see this woman has been through something terrible and is about to collapse?"

Haggie sat there for a second. "But the sofa," he said, pointing ineffectually.

Mona glared at him. "Haggie." The woman's legs started to curve beneath her. Haggie put one hand on each arm of the chair and hoisted himself up, wobbling a bit on his feet.

"Where are you from?" Mona asked, leaning down to re-lace the top of her right boot.

The woman closed her eyes. "Sinai," she said. Haggie sat on the floor.

"What did she say?" Mona whispered, relacing the left boot for the hell of it. "Did she say cyanide?"

He looked up and noticed the woman was already asleep.

"Faster than me, even," he said with respect.

"Do you think she's a poisoner?" Mona hissed.

Haggie laughed.

"Sssh," said Mona, "she's sleeping."

"Her dress is burnt," he said.

"I know," said Mona, "she smells like smoke, too. Camp-fire smoke or something." She stood up. "Listen, Hag, I've got to go. Are you okay? Should I stay? What if she poisons you?"

Haggie made an attempt at a scared face but he couldn't get himself to do it. He felt too tired. "Go, Mona," he said. He laid his head back on the arm of the sofa.

Mona paused. "Do you think she's sick?"

"She's just tired." His voice was fading. "She just needs

some sleep." The sofa arm dug into his neck. "I can't believe she wanted to give you her ring."

Mona smiled and checked herself one last time in the mirror. As soon as the front door closed and the clop-clop of her tightly laced boots faded away, Haggie tried to doze off, but the floor was hard beneath him and the air felt clotted and thick without Mona stirring it up, and he couldn't find the familiar relief of that slow descending weight.

Heaving himself up, he sat on the couch. He almost twitched, craving the comfort of his chair. The woman snored lightly now. She had flushed skin and her eyelashes made simple black arcs on her cheeks.

"Hello lady," said Haggie, "wake up and talk to me." She kept sleeping, sending out her breath to the air and pulling it back in. Private.

It made him feel worse to be awake when there was someone else there that was asleep. The house seemed twice as big and twice as lonely. Dragging himself up, Haggie lumbered over to the bathroom. He wondered: was it possible to die simply from an absence of tempo? Sure, Mona was ruled by some kind of frenetic march, but there was no doubt that *something* was moving her inside—Haggie's internal rhythms were so slow that he wondered if they counted as rhythms at all.

Inside the bathroom, he opened up the medicine cabinet above the sink; sometimes Mona kept sleeping pills in there that she used when she was too wound up. Which was often. Holding the mirrored door, Haggie took down the tiny red-brown bottle. He read the label. *Do not exceed two in six hours.* Haggie spilled them out on his hand; they shimmered like miniature moons. I'm bigger than she is, besides, he thought. He took nine, his lucky number, and washed them down with a handful of water from the tap. That should do something, he thought. Because I don't have my chair. And I'm tired, he thought again. I'm very tired and I want to sleep. He sat down on the floor of the bathroom and waited for a strange feeling to overtake him. The woman in his chair stopped snoring and the house filled with darkness and quiet.

4.

When he had finished exploring every knob and bump in the frame, he took in a breath and got ready to face the mirror straight on. He fiddled with the itchy gold necklace. This time would be different, in this fancy man's mirror, this good-looking man's looking glass. He crossed his fingers inside the chain and let his eyes shift in and focus.

5. At the Side of the Road

That night, I sleep in a bush. I don't sleep very well there, but I never do, I've never been a good sleeper. I can't ever get comfortable. So it's okay; the dirt on my cheek is okay, doesn't make any difference to me. A pillow is no better.

I dream about my husband. I am dreaming that he is going to the refrigerator to fix himself a sandwich, my food, my bread, my self—digested then gone—and that's when the shot rings out and that's when I'm off, in the race, I'm off. He grabs his knee, and I'm out the door. I'm a racer, I'm so fast. In my dream, I run a lap around the world and some people in another country build a monument around my footprint.

When I wake up, I want to walk for a long time, I think I could walk forever and never get tired. I take one of the cigarettes that man left me and smoke it, it's been a long time since I did that, and when I stub it out in the bush, it catches on something and the bush starts to burn. Just near the bottom, but it is burning, the bush is on fire. The air is dry, sure, but it was one tiny cigarette and so I am shocked and I look at the bush burn and then I think: maybe this is something spiritual. Here, by the side of the road, just me without any money, just me wanting a new place to go, this is the time for something spiritual to happen, this is my right timing. I wait for God to speak to me.

The flames snap and hiss.

A couple drivers pass by and slow: Want a Ride? but I shake my head, no, and it's not because I'm worried about rapists, I'm not. Something is about to happen here—something big. I'm going to hear what this bush has to say to me and then I'm going to walk forever by myself since I never have and because it's a better quiet outside than it is in a car and because all I took was one puff and I set something on fire. Me. The bush keeps crackling. I wonder, what will it tell me? What is it that I need to hear? I lean in closer and listen with my whole being. I can't tell what it's saying. I can't find any words, just that fire sound, the sound of cracking and bursting. I start to feel a bit panicked—what if it speaks in a different language? What would I do then? The warmth of the flames flushes my face.

I speak English, I whisper to the bush as a reminder. Talk to me. I'm listening.

6.

Same ugly man.

7. Back at Haggie and Mona's

At one in the morning, a key turned in the lock and Mona tiptoed into the living room. She could see the shape of the woman still there, lungs lifting and releasing. She felt a surge of pride that the runaway was alive and had stayed, and eased herself down on the couch across from the woman and un- laced her boots.

It had been a great date. He'd been one of those men who kissed hard, trying to merge their faces. Hand at the back of her head. It was quite urgent kissing for a first date but she liked that. She left the boots by the couch, tiptoed into the bathroom and flipped on the light and there was Haggie lying on the floor, legs tucked into his chest.

"Haggie," she said, stopping still, "what's going on?"

He craned his head and looked up at her with enormous eyes.

"I committed suicide," he said. "But it didn't work."

"What?" Mona squatted on the floor.

"I mean," he said, "I just wanted to sleep and sleep, sleep and sleep, so I took nine pills, nine dangerous white pills, those pills you use to sleep sometimes? I took them hours ago. Hours and hours ago. Nine of them. I'm sure of it. And I feel fine."

She stared at him. "Did you puke?"

"No," he said, "I didn't even puke."

"Haggie," she said, "are you okay?" She reached forward and felt his forehead. "You're not feverish," she said. She sat down next to him. "Are you okay?"

"I think so," he said.

She stared at him still. He stared back. Standing up, Mona pulled the bottle down from the medicine cabinet and read the label. She looked down at him and shook her head. "Nine?" she asked, and he nodded. She kept shaking her head, placing the bottle back on the shelf and closing the door. Then she squatted down next to him again and touched his hair. Her voice was quiet. "I'm worried about you," she said.

"I know." He reached up an arm to grasp the counter. "Me too." He pulled himself up. "But still, it's all so strange."

Mona grasped his elbow. "Do you need help walking?"

"No." He shook his head. "That's the thing. I don't."

He walked into the living room and stood against the back of the stiff sofa, facing the big window that looked out onto their small backyard. Mona followed him in.

"She's still here," she whispered, pointing.

"Did you have a good date?" Haggie looked at the woman sleeping. Her entire face was relaxed. He thought she looked beautiful.

"Yeah," she said, "it was really nice. He liked the boots." Haggie smiled. "Are you going to sleep?"

"I guess not yet," he said, "I'm feeling pretty awake right now. I think I'll just stay in here."

"Okay." She touched his shoulder. "You're sure you're okay?"

He nodded. "I'm good," he said. "Good night, Mone. Sleep well."

Mona picked up her boots and pattered into her bedroom. The woman shifted in the chair. Haggie went over to her and gently rolled the chair forward until they both were in front of the window. He looked at their reflections silhouetted in the glass. She still smelled like smoke and it smelled good. He remembered Mona: what if she poisons you? and smiled. He sat on the arm of the couch and watched their undetailed shapes in the glass. Once Mona went to the bathroom. Other than that, it was perfectly still. After several hours, sunlight began to seep into the backyard, slowly opening out the flatness of the glass and revealing the grass and one tree. A dew-covered white plastic chair. An empty wooden bird feeder.

He watched as their silhouettes faded from the window and dissipated into the morning.

8.

He started to cry, same ugly man, always: that tidal wave of disappointment. Transformation impossible. He pulled the itchy fake gold necklace off and threw it at the glass where it made an unsatisfying clink; he let out a small, ineffective spit which didn't land on the mirror at all but instead arced down and splatted onto the fancy silver frame. The muttering man started to rub the spit into the frame, but as he did, the saliva seemed to remove a bit of the silver. "What?" he said out loud. He leaned forward. He rubbed more. Silver paint lifted off, thin and papery. Beneath it was scarred wood. The muttering man licked his finger and rubbed again. The paint continued to peel off. Darkened silver, iridescent black, collected under his fingernails, on the tops of his fingertips. Ignoring his face, he hunched down and kept rubbing. What do you know, he said, mutter mutter, well who would've thought it was a fake frame too. He rubbed the entire frame until his hands were black and it was no longer silver at all, but just a rectangle of flawed bumpy brown wood.

Turning the mirror around, he opened up the hooks and removed the glass from the back. Then he hung the frame around his neck. "Will you look at my new necklace," he said out loud, to the empty street. "This one doesn't itch at all."

95

9. Mine

I sit with the bush for a long time but it says nothing to me. It continues to burn, still mainly near the bottom. I listen harder and harder, feeling a certain despair build, wondering if it will ever reach out and talk, if ever I will understand the message meant for me, but then, just as I'm listening as hard as I possibly can, it hits me, pow, like that: of course. It is saying nothing. It's a listening bush. It wants me to talk. My burning bush would be different, my burning bush would be like me.

So I clear my throat and I tell it things, I talk to that bush. I don't think I've ever said so many sentences in a row before, but I talk for at least an hour about myself—about me and my husband and my mother and my allergies, and sometimes I don't know what to say and then I just describe what I see. The street is gray and paved. The ground is dry here. The sky is cloudless.

It's wonderful. It's wonderful to talk like that. After a while, I'm exhausted and I think I've said enough. I feel great but my throat is dry and I need some water, so, thanking it over and over, I leave the burning bush by the side of the road for somebody else. And I start to walk.

It's hours later when hunger and fatigue hit, and I find myself in front of one house, the only house on the block without bars on its windows. That's the one I knock at. And that's the one that answers. It's a nice place. It is quiet inside. Just as I'm dozing off, ready to really sleep for the first time in a long time, I think about my husband and where he is, what he's doing. I like to think he's limping around the house, shouting my name, sitting on the bed and looking where the mirror was and staring at the grain of the wood. I like to think he opens the refrigerator and sees me inside.

But truthfully? Let me tell you what I honestly think.

I think, maybe he hasn't even noticed that I'm gone.

But. I have.

DRUNKEN MIMI

There was an imp that went to high school with stilts on so that no one would know he was an imp. Of course he never wore shorts.

He bugged the girls; he had a few friends whose parents were drug addicts; he was the greatest at parties—he'd take any dare. He propositioned mothers. He told stories about airplane sex. He claimed he knew everything about women. They were all fifteen; no one dared contest that.

One thing he didn't know was that there was a mermaid at the school; she was a sophomore as well. She wore long skirts that swept the floor and one large boot covering her tail and she used a crutch, pretending like her second leg, which of course didn't exist, was hurt.

She was a quiet one, that mermaid; she excelled in ocean-ography class, but she also made an effort to not be *too* good; she didn't want to call attention to herself. On every test she

missed at least three. *(What is plankton?* A boat, she wrote.)
She was very beautiful; hair slightly greenish which everyone
attributed to chlorine. Eyes purplish which everyone attributed to drugs. The girls called her a snob. The boys shoved
each other and agreed.

The imp sat behind her in the one class they shared: English. He had a perpetual monologue of jokes going on under
his breath. Did you hear the one about the square egg? he'd
say to himself, laughing at the punch line before it even happened. Often, it never happened anyway. One day he reached
forward and dipped a strand of her long mossy hair into his
beer. He snuck beer into class, no problem. He was a clever
imp. He'd poured it into a Coke can.

What he didn't know was that her hair had nerves; it was
different than human hair; it was not dead skin; it was alive.
The mermaid felt the change instantly and woozed with con-
tentment: liquid. Lifting. Home.

Had the imp lifted the can, he would've been stunned: it
was so light! Where did the beer go? Had he looked closer, he
might've seen it riding up the strands of her hair, brown
droplets on a lime escalator, sucked up by that straw of a lock,
foam vanishing into the mane in front of him, the mane he
pictured at night floating over his small shoulders when he
was in his bed, naked, eyes closed.

Snob queen. Hair green. Mine.

The mermaid got drunk off the beer. She had very low
tolerance. There was no alcohol allowed underwater.

That day, she exited English class swaying. The imp picked

it up right away; he thought: man, she's a party girl, too! She's perfect! Drunken Mimi!

He worried about taking off his clothes. He worried about her hand, grazing to his knee—what are these wooden poles doing where your shins should be? she'd ask. She'd have a puzzled look in those purpled eyes. Snob, he'd think. He worried, but still, he tracked her through the halls; the way she leaned, hard on this drunken day, was sexy. The way she trusted the crutch. He tracked her one huge boot.

It was lunchtime. The mermaid wandered off to lie down under the orange-red bleachers. Her head felt bleary. Her hair felt alive. When she let it stray out into the dirt, her hair coughed. She put her backpack under her head and that was better.

The imp found her there. He wasn't sure what to say.

Did you hear the one about the man with one leg? he began. Then he felt stupid right away. Bad choice.

The mermaid looked up.

Excuse me? she said.

The imp sat down next to her, arranging his stilts.

So, he said. A guy walks into a bar.

She turned her head slightly toward him, but said nothing.

He lay down next to her. The dirt was flat and fine, and he picked up a discarded cigarette butt and began digging a hole to put it in.

The imp was nervous; he hoped no one was sitting above them, on the bleachers, eavesdropping. That tall guy? they'd say. He's not nearly as smooth as he says he is.

I like your hair, he said then.

Thank you, said the mermaid. She paused. She looked at him for a long second. Then she said: You can touch it if you want to.

Really? The imp wanted nothing more.

Really, said the mermaid. She gave him a lip smile. Just be gentle.

The imp left the half-buried cigarette butt and reached his hand forward to stroke down the fine green strands.

Soft, he said.

The mermaid shivered. Each hair delivered a tiny note of murmurings all the way down through her.

The imp started at the root and let his hand ride the sheen all the way to the ends.

So did you hear the one about the dead cat? he said, giggling a little.

The mermaid didn't answer; her eyes were closing.

See there's this cat, the imp began, and it gets hit by a car. And when it goes up to heaven, St. Peter asks it why he should let it into heaven.

I know you're an imp, said the mermaid.

His hand paused.

Don't stop, she said. Please.

How did you know, he wailed, no one knows! He pictured the police. He pictured the PA announcement. He clutched her hair for a second, inadvertently.

Ouch, said the mermaid. Gentle please.

Will you bust me? asked the imp.

Of course not, said the mermaid. I like imps, she said.

You do?

Definitely, she said. Imps are sweet.

Sweet? Sweet? He touched her arm.

No, she said. Just the hair.

He twitched and coughed. Stroked her hair again, slower now. Her face was starting to flush, a slow reddening.

It's my secret, he said. She said, I understand.

He said, I'm not so sweet.

Her hair was growing staticky; it clung to his fingers.

Okay, he said, and he giggled again. Okay, he said, so the cat, the dead cat, it tells St. Peter it's been a good cat, it brought mice to its owner for many years, said the imp.

His legs turned in and out, the stilts brittle bones beneath his blue jeans. He kept stroking her hair. Root to end. Root to end.

St. Peter, continued the imp, so St. Peter sends the cat to hell because it's a killer.

He paused, hand in the middle of her head.

Don't stop, she said again.

Root to end. Hair curved around his fingers in soft coils.

Your hair is pretty, he said.

She was quiet. Her hair lifted off the backpack onto his hand, a cloth of pale pale green, a curtain rising.

The imp's hand was steady but his fingers were trembling now. Okay, he continued. So. In hell, the devil said: Catch me some mice, killer cat! I want to cook them in my stew!

But the cat said No. It said I won't do that for you, devil. I only kill mice for a good master; I won't kill any mice for you.

And poof! The cat went straight up to heaven.

The imp giggled. He looked down at the mermaid.

That's it, he said. That's the joke.

Root to end.

I made it up, he said.

Her eyes were closed; her breath was faster.

Mimi, said the imp, are you okay?

Don't stop, she said again, barely breathing, please, she said, keep going. He kept stroking down, watching close, what was going on?, and when her back finally curled up, breath out in puffs, he didn't stop even then, he was steady and quiet and watching, he was root to end, until finally she reached up her hand, breathless, and grabbed his, holding on so tightly, thanking him over and over, not snobby at all, not snobby at all, thank you, thank you, until he laughed out loud in surprise. Her purple eyes were purpler and he thought he smelled flowers.

FELL THIS
GIRL

On my way to work I see this woman wearing a short shirt that shows her belly button. She has a rounded stomach, and the skin curving in makes her belly button look like a very deep hole. I'm walking with my Walkman on down Steiner, music loud in my ears for a Friday morning, and I feel a wave of desire to stick my dick in that deep dark belly button hole, to fuck the woman with the short shirt, to lay her down on the sidewalk and take her. She walks by and I walk by and I continue on my way to work.

Of course nothing happens. But I can imagine so clearly what it's like to enter a woman, I feel like I've done it. My body is on hers, drunk off the conquest, sliding in slow: my hips, push, the glaze. I think about that belly button girl and I think I would shock her and I like that. I want to see girls melt because girls are so goddamn elusive, you can't tell what the fuck they're thinking, except I am a girl, and I know just what a lot of girls are thinking, I know what I'm thinking, and right now it's exactly this.

I go to a party and sit around with people I don't know very well or like and we talk about movies we all hated. I am wearing a short skirt that flows, and a shirt with a scoop neck and I am luscious. I meet a man at this party who walks me back to my car. He has shaggy red hair, and calluses on his fingers from construction, or guitar, or golf; viva la mystery— I do not ask.

By the car I take his hand and I lay it on my breast. I'm feeling very bold since I had three beers and all I really want right now is this warm callused mysterious hand on me. He seems taken aback, but then his face lightens and his other arm reaches out to hold my waist, and I melt, I melt, I open up like a dream and I'm his for the night until the warmth goes cold.

He is a bad kisser, but he has very fine hands. We're in the Mission and he happens to live just a few blocks away on Valencia so we go to his room which has curved-out Victorian windows and a bed on the floor and a poster of a band I've never heard of called Swat and next to the poster there is a flyswatter hanging on the wall signed by the band and I think it's sort of cool. He kisses the back of my neck, and I change my mind and decide he's a good kisser, and our clothes come off in the way that clothes do, and it's semidark in his room, and I, for the moment, never want to leave.

He tells me nice things about my body.

While he fucks me, I imagine fucking some woman, my

mouth set in a grim way. It's the three of us in bed: me the woman, me the man, and him, the red-haired guy with the great hands. He thinks I'm just some girly girl, receptacle envelope girl, he doesn't know what I'm thinking. He doesn't know that I'm also a shadow on his back, pushing in.

"Oh," he keeps saying over and over, "oh," and his eyes are closed in concentration. When we sleep together, he holds me like he loves me. I've noticed this: when it's the first date, and you fuck, the guy holds you much better than he does the next few times. The first date, you're sort of the stand-in for whomever he loved last, before he fully realizes you're not her, and so you get all this nice residue emotion. I felt cherished, tucked into his belly, like we'd known each other for years and I was his wonderful girl and we both slept great.

The red-haired guy's name is, of course, Patrick.

Before he wakes up I run to the bathroom to see what I look like, and I actually look pretty good. Flushed and fuck-able. I go back and he's still sprawled out on the bed and I fold my body back into his and think about how I want to look to him when he wakes up. I want to be sleeping in a casual sexy way, to make him want me again.

I remember, especially in high school, I was so good at this kind of fake-out. I rehearsed thoughtfulness, I appeared care-free—and how many guys did I trick? As I sat there, hair tucked behind my ear, supposedly lost in a book, thinking this exact monologue, rereading and rereading the same paragraph, waiting for them to see me and want me, caught in this image of myself as a reader. What about staring at ants, wanting to seem close to nature and whimsical? What about staring into space, wanting to seem expansive, trying to find the thoughts that would fit my self-portrait? I fooled so many guys! I was found mysterious so many times, oh that girl, we don't know what that Susie thinks, and all I'm thinking is what do I look like, and all I'm thinking is that I own their thoughts.

Curled into Patrick, I end up falling asleep again anyway, and when I wake up he's across the room. I run my finger over the titles in his bookshelf and find a photo album. It's pretty heavy but I lift it into bed and start flipping through it.

"Patrick," I say, "who's in these pictures?"

He's sorting through videotapes maybe because he wants to watch something. He glances up.

"Friends, old girlfriends, you know, photo album stuff." The morning light is on his back and he looks pale and beautiful.

"So who's the most important girlfriend of all these people?" I ask. I can see several women in the pictures, and they're all attractive which makes me feel both good and bad.

"What do you mean the most important?" He has a yawn in his voice, but I think he's faking.

"You know, the one you really loved."

He walks over to me, leaving a pile of videotapes, and flips through the stiff photo album pages fast, and then I know he knows the order really well and that he likes to look at his photos and it makes me want to glue myself to his body.

"Here," he says, pointing. There are a few photos of a brunette with short hair and a big, smiling mouth, Patrick and the brunette at the Grand Canyon, Patrick and the brunette taking a self-timer picture so that their faces are distorted and their noses look huge.

"That's the one you loved?"

He nods and leaves the room. He leaves the videotapes all over the floor. I study the girl. She does not look a thing like me. He doesn't come back in for a while, and then I hear the rustle of the newspaper and I know I've lost him for at least an hour. I pick up the phone and call my sister Eleanor. She'll be up early on a Saturday morning. She has nothing else to do.

"Hello?" Her voice is lower than mine, and sounds like the voice of an older woman.

"Ellie, do you think I should cut my hair short?" I'm naked and I stick my legs up into the air because they look the best that way, all the skin slides up and creates muscles.

"Susie, whatever." Eleanor is always depressed. Eleanor is fat.

"I think I'm tired of the way I'm looking. Do you want to go shopping with me? It's early, but maybe later on today?" I love to go shopping with Eleanor because in contrast I look so great in everything.

"I work," she says.

"Is Mom there?" I ask.

"Yeah, do you want to talk to her?"

"No," I say, "but will you ask her if she thinks I'd look good in short hair?" There's a pause while I hear Eleanor ask the question like a good big sister. The tiredness in her voice should make me feel bad but it doesn't. What it makes me want to do is go take a karate class because I like to hold my hands like that and chopping up a board would feel good—smash, the crack, the thud.

Eleanor says Mom doesn't care. I say goodbye and hang up the phone. I go into the kitchen and have an English muffin without asking and read parts of the paper with the glamorous people and Patrick looks up and smiles at one point which is very smart of him if he ever wants to see my ass in bed again.

Turns out Patrick is working underneath the city inside a pothole, fixing pipes or something. He gets to lift up the pothole and jump inside. I laugh, I tell him it's like he's fucking the city with his whole body but he doesn't get it, and I think when he doesn't get something he's just quiet. In fact, he's usually quiet. In fact, I talk mostly all the time around Patrick, or anyone.

I go to find him inside the pothole. He told me it was on Divisadero and they don't reclose the pothole, so there it is, like some hobbit door, opened up to anybody. I slip down into the belly of the street which is incredibly exciting, and it's dark and it smells pretty awful and I can hear the cars rushing by above me. They seem like they're going really fucking *fast*.

"Hey Patrick," I yell, "hey Patrick, you have guests." My voice booms out through the passages, and after a while I hear a rustling and it's Patrick wearing something orange and he does not look happy to see me.

"What are you doing here?" He's gruff, like his boss is next to him or something, but as far as I can tell, we're alone.

"I thought I'd come bring you a plant for your new house," I say, laughing, wishing I *had* brought a plant and thinking about how witty I am and why doesn't he love me yet.

"You need to go, Susie," he says. "It's totally unsafe for you to be here. You need a special permit." He won't even look at me. His hands are gloved and the gloves are covered with oil. I want him to grab me with those gloves and smear oil all over my body and my nice dress and throw me on the ground, with all these cars above us, a ceiling of cars.

"Susie. Go." His voice is louder now, almost mean. I start to climb back and he puts his hands on my thighs to help hoist me up and I swear it turns me on so much that I practically drop back in there but I want to see Patrick again, and if I did that, I bet he'd lock his doors to me forever.

Back on the street, the cars seem really slow. The air is bright and I can still smell oil in my nose. I have nothing to do and it's Saturday night almost and I don't think Patrick is going to want to see me first thing when he exits the pothole.

I go to a bar and have a beer. The bartender doesn't look at me and instead talks a lot to the girl next to me who has a perfect ponytail, and I eat a bag of pretzels and then rip the bag into ribbons. The whole experience only takes half an hour, and I'm sick of being ignored, so I leave.

I walk up the street with beer taste in my mouth, warm and bitter and wonderful, and what do you know, there's that girl again, the belly button girl, leaning back to show that marvelous hole to the world. She has no fucking idea.

When I walk past her, I want to grab her wrist and drag her down into the pothole, which is just a block or two back. She looks at me and smiles because she knows she has nothing to fear from me, she thinks I'm her ally, but I'm not. I really want to trample down this girl who has her belly button open wide like it's there just for me. I want to hurt her because she looks like she might be happy and she might have a date and if she doesn't, she will. I want to fuck her by a Dumpster and cut her down, like she's a tree, I don't care if she wants me back, I don't care if so many people back home love her so much. I walk and I walk and I walk and I end up at Mount Zion Hospital which means I'm near my mom's house and I go by the house and in the upstairs window I can see a hint of Eleanor, in front of the TV, with potato chips. I don't really want to touch Eleanor. Mostly I just want her to wake up. Wake up! I feel like pouring water on her a lot. I keep walking; I don't want to talk to my sister and I definitely don't want to see my mom.

I pass a haircutter which is a stay-open-late haircutter for last-minute urges. It's just closing and I go in and ask her to cut all my hair off until it's really short and sassy, and she's so tired and beat and I bet she has five kids or something, but she does it anyway, in like ten minutes. She charges me ten bucks, a buck a minute I guess. It looks not good. I keep checking out my silhouette in the windows of stores and shaking my head to make sure the reflection is me. When I touch the back of my neck, it feels nice. I walk in zigzags through the side streets until I hit a fancy hotel and wander in and there is a knot of old rich men and I go up to them.

"Anyone want to buy me a drink?" I ask, and they all smile and they all want to, but none of them do, they sort of shake their heads in unison like they're old ducks. I plop down on the red velveteen hotel couch and another older man comes up to me.

"I overheard you," he says, "and I'd love to buy you a drink."

I smile up at him. He has gray hair, but he's quite handsome.

"Great. Whatever you want to get me." I lean back on the couch and close my eyes while he's off at the bar. When he returns, I want to appear the image of ease and raw sexuality. I open my legs so there's just a hint of darkness at the crotch. I lay my arms across the top of the couch like I'm claiming the world, this is all mine, I'm so confident. He returns with a vodka something for me, ten degrees below zero, the glass is frosted up and it slides down like very cold, watery-tasting water. I'm drunk in five minutes.

He asks me questions which I lie about and then wants to know if I want to come up into his hotel room which is a few floors up and I'm not really sure if I want to, but I do.

It's on the ninth floor and it's a suite. It's really nice, with gold antique faucets and no lame landscape paintings on the wall, and a view of the bridge and the city lights which are just now coming on, ten by ten.

He stands behind me and unzips my dress, just like that, and I close my eyes and imagine he's Patrick. Right now, Patrick is probably wondering where I am and maybe is very sorry because he made me feel so bad in the pothole or maybe he never wants to see me again because he thinks I'm some nut who goes into potholes, and maybe he's right because here I am in a hotel about to fuck a rich businessman who really, in fact, could be my father.

I keep my eyes closed and feel his hands all over me and I think about his body, if it will be wrinkled with gray chest hairs, and I want to cut his throat with a long sharp knife and that gets me wet.

"This is such a nice surprise," he says. "I didn't expect this from my vacation."

I don't say anything. My eyes are still closed. He kisses me and it's an okay kiss and he holds my face and smells nice and there's a door in me that opens and I feel like I could cry and I could crawl inside his wrinkled-up gray chest and cry and it feels like he took his hand and somehow stuck it through my heart.

I need to go, but I don't. He guides me toward the bed,

and all my energy right now is concentrated on not crying. I don't even notice when he takes off my clothes and lays me down and I'm just practicing my breathing, one two three, in out. Don't cry, crying would be bad, but there is a whole cyclone of tears swirling in my throat and I just try to break it down, go away, piece by piece back into my stomach. I put my hands on his arms and the skin slides up a little because he's this old man, so I decide with my eyes still closed that he's Eleanor and she lost all this weight and so now her skin doesn't fit anymore. He's Eleanor and she's tucking me in as she did when I was little and Dad left and I kept thinking he would come in through the window and trip over something and die, trying to get me back, and Eleanor would stroke my forehead and tell me there was nothing he could trip on; she would clear the path by the window. I loved my sister so much, that she didn't laugh at me, that she cleared the path instead. And it makes me want to cry again, my love for Eleanor, and the tears sort of gather while my eyes are closed and I grip those arms and move my hips and I feel so proud of my Eleanor for losing all this weight. And when her skin bounces back to fit her body, oh she will be so beautiful. How I would love it if she would be the beautiful one for a while and I could slide into the background and be ugly and quiet.

His breathing has changed, I barely noticed the way he came in a pleased grunt. He slides off me, hand lingering on my hip. I've been waiting for this break so that I could run into the bathroom.

I open my eyes. His face is right there, redder and sweaty, a sappy smile on his face and I politely fake a smile back and excuse myself and go into the antique gold faucets and the little plastic bottles of hotel shampoo and sit on the toilet. For a second, I think I might split down the middle and reveal a six-year-old mess, like a Russian doll except we don't match. But I don't, the moment is over, I feel a few tears dribble down but the rush of them that I was swallowing is gone now. I'm just me in my body on the toilet, looking at myself in the mirror with my new short hair that is all messed up.

He's asleep when I leave, let myself out the door and down the elevator and through the streets to my own apartment. It's dark and there are no messages on the answering machine, the red light is steady. No one has called me. Patrick has not called me, and we were supposed to have plans tonight.

I stand in front of the mirror and I look at my body in this little dress I'm wearing, and my socks folding over different lengths and I try and forget that I just fucked a sixty-five-year-old man who only bought me one drink. I think about that whole dick fantasy, and I try to get myself to want to fuck myself. Here you go, I say, look at that fine ass, look at that body, you want to take her don't you, you want to fell this girl.

But I just see some girl in a blue dress with short hair and sad eyes and I really don't want to fuck her at all. She looks so tired to me. I go to the window and look out at the lights of the city which are every color and I stick my head out. It's pretty windy, so it throws my hair back and I feel like a dog riding in a car and the wind is cold and brings tears to my eyes and I try to pretend they're sad tears and sniffle a little.

The night is mostly quiet and I can only hear the sounds of things far away. After a while a cab pulls up downstairs. It honks and three girls come out of my building in little skirts and shiny hair and they get in the cab and they're already laughing. The wind keeps pulling tears from my eyes. I'm poised like a gargoyle above them and I think about letting myself fall out the window and landing on the top of the cab to go where they're going. Bending the metal of the roof until it presses down hard on one of the girls' heads and she panics and yells at the driver who doesn't listen. Help, she says to her friends, something's going on, the car is caving in! They think she's kidding but it's real: there is a mass that is me on top of her, watching the lights and the sky pass me by in a rush, pushing down on that metal until I'm crushing her skull. My ass and her brain. My weight and her burden. I will close my eyes and feel the speed. I will feel the wind fill up my dress and pass through me in tunnels until I am so numb with cold, I can't tell when we stop.

PART THREE

THE HEALER

There were two mutant girls in the town: one had a hand made of fire and the other had a hand made of ice. Everyone else's hands were normal. The girls first met in elementary school and were friends for about three weeks. Their parents were delighted; the mothers in particular spent hours on the phone describing over and over the shock of delivery day.

I remember one afternoon, on the playground, the fire girl grabbed hold of the ice girl's hand and—Poof—just like that, each equalized the other. Their hands dissolved into regular flesh—exit mutant, enter normal. The fire girl panicked and let go, finding that her fire reblazed right away, while the ice spun back fast around the other girl's fingers like a cold glass turban. They grasped hands again; again, it worked. Delighted by the neat new trick, I think they even charged money to perform it for a while and made a pretty penny.

Audiences loved to watch the two little girls dabbling in the elements with their tiny powerful fists.

After a while, the ice girl said she was tired of the trick and gave it up and they stopped being friends. I'd never seen them together since but now they were both sixteen and in the same science class. I was there too; I was a senior then.

The fire girl sat in the back row. Sparks dripped from her fingertips like sweat and fizzed on the linoleum. She looked both friendly and lonely. After school, she was most popular with the cigarette kids who found her to be the coolest of lighters.

The ice girl sat in the front row and wore a ponytail. She kept her ice hand in her pocket but you knew it was there because it leaked. I remember when the two met, at the start of the school year, face-to-face for the first time in years, the fire girl held out her fire hand, I guess to try the trick again, but the ice girl shook her head. I'm not a shaker, she said. Those were her exact words. I could tell the fire girl felt bad. I gave her a sympathetic look but she missed it. After school let out, she passed along the brick wall, lighting cigarette after cigarette, tiny red circles in a line. She didn't keep the smokers company; just did her duty and then walked home, alone.

Our town was ringed by a circle of hills and because of this no one really came in and no one ever left. Only one boy made it out. He'd been very gifted at public speech and one afternoon he climbed over Old Midge, the shortest of the ring, and vanished forever. After six months or so he mailed his mother a postcard with a fish on it that said: In the Big City. Giving Speeches All Over. Love, J. She Xeroxed the postcard and gave every citizen a copy. I stuck it on the wall by my bed. I made up his speeches, regularly, on my way to school; they always involved me. *Today we focus on Lisa,* J.'s voice would sail out, *Lisa with the two flesh hands.* This is generally where I'd stop— I wasn't sure what to add.

During science class that fall, the fire girl burnt things with her fingers. She entered the room with a pile of dry leaves in her book bag and by the time the bell rang, there was ash all over her desk. She seemed to need to do this. It prevented some potential friendships, however, because most people were too scared to approach her. I tried but I never knew what to say. For Christmas that year I bought her a log. Here, I said, I got this for you to burn up. She started to cry. I said: Do you hate it? but she said No. She said it was a wonderful gift and from then on she remembered my name.

I didn't buy anything for the ice girl. What do you get an ice girl anyway? She spent most of her non-school time at the hospital, helping sick people. She was a great soother, they said. Her water had healing powers.

What happened was the fire girl met Roy. And that's when everything changed.

I found them first, and it was accidental, and I told no one, so it wasn't my fault. Roy was a boy who had no parents and lived alone. He was very rarely at school and he was a cutter. He cut things into his skin with a razor blade. I saw once;

some Saturday when everyone was at a picnic and I was bored, I wandered into the boys' bathroom and he was in there and he showed me how he carved letters into his skin. He'd spelled out OUCH on his leg. Raised and white. I put out a hand and touched it and then I walked directly home. It was hard to feel those letters. They still felt like skin.

I don't know exactly how the fire girl met Roy but they spent their afternoons by the base of the mountains and she would burn him. A fresh swatch of skin every day. I was on a long walk near Old Midge after school, wondering if I'd ever actually cross it, when I passed the two of them for the first time. I almost waved and called out Hi but then I saw what was going on. Her back was to me, but still I could see that she was leaning forward with one fire finger pressed against his inner elbow and his eyes were shut and he was moaning. The flames hissed and crisped on contact. She sucked in her breath, sss, and then she pulled her hand away and they both crumpled back, breathing hard. Roy had a new mark on his arm. This one did not form a letter. It swirled into itself, black and detailed, a tiny whirlpool of lines.

I turned and walked away. My own hands were shaking. I had to force myself to leave instead of going back and watching more. I kept walking until I looped the entire town.

All during the next month, both Roy and the fire girl looked really happy. She stopped bringing leaves into science class and started participating and Roy smiled at me in the street which had *never* happened before. I continued my mountain walks after school, and usually I'd see them pressed into the shade, but I never again allowed myself to stop and watch. I didn't want to invade their privacy but it was more than that; something about watching them reminded me of quicksand, slide and pull in, as fast as that. I just took in what I could as I passed by. It always smelled a bit like barbecue, where they were. This made me hungry, which made me uncomfortable.

It was some family, off to the base of Old Midge to go camping, that saw and told everyone.

The fire girl is hurting people! they announced, and Roy tried to explain but his arms and thighs were pocked with fingerprint scars and it said OUCH in writing on his thigh and no one believed him, they believed the written word instead, and placed him in a foster home. I heard he started chewing glass.

They put the fire girl in jail. She's a danger, everyone said, she burns things, she burns people. She likes it. This was true: at the jail she grabbed the forearm of the guard with her fire fist and left a smoking tarantula handprint; he had to go to the hospital and be soothed by the ice girl.

The whole town buzzed about the fire girl all week. They said: She's crazy! Or: She's primitive! I lay in my bed at night, and thought of her concentrating and leaning in to Roy. I thought of her shuddering out to the trees like a drum.

I went to the burn ward and found the ice girl. If anyone, I thought, she might have some answers.

She was holding her hand above a sick man in a bed with red sores all over his body, and her ice was dripping into his mouth and he looked thrilled.

I want you to come to the jail, I said, and give her a little relief.

The ice girl looked over at me. Who are you? she asked.

I was annoyed. I'm in your science class, I said, Lisa.

She gave a nod. Oh right, she said. You sit in the middle.

I looked at the man in the hospital bed, the bliss on his face, the gloom on hers.

This can't be too fun for you, I said.

She didn't answer. Come to the jail, I said, please, she's so unhappy, maybe you can help.

The ice girl checked the watch on her flesh hand. The man beneath her made something close to a purring sound. If you come back in an hour, she said at last, I'll go for a little bit.

Thank you, I said, this is another good deed.

She raised her slim eyebrows. I have enough good deeds, she said. It's just that I've never seen the jail.

I returned in exactly an hour, and we went over together.

The guard at the jail beamed at the ice girl. My wife had cancer, he said, and you fixed her up just fine. The ice girl smiled. Her smile was small. I asked where the fire girl was and the guard pointed. Careful, he said, she's nutso. He coughed and crossed his legs. We turned to his point, and I led the way down.

The fire girl was at the back of her cell, burning up

the fluffy inside of the mattress. She recognized me right away.

Hi, Lisa, she said, how's it going?

Fine, I said. We're on frogs now in science.

She nodded. The ice girl stood back, looking around at the thick stone walls and the low ceiling. The room was dank and smelled moldy.

Look who I brought, I said. Maybe she can help you.

The fire girl looked up. Hey, she said. They exchanged a nod. It was all so formal. I was annoyed. It seems to me that in a jail, you don't need to be that formal, you can let some things loose.

So, wanting to be useful, I went right over to the ice girl and pulled her hand out of her pocket, against her half-protests. I held it forward, and stuck it through the bars of the cell. It was surprisingly heavy which filled me with new sympathy. It felt like a big cold rock.

Here, I said, shaking it a little, go to it.

The fire girl grasped the ice girl's hand. I think we weren't sure it would work, if the magic had worn off in junior high, but it hadn't; as soon as they touched, the ice melted away and the fire burned out and they were just two girls holding hands through the bars of a jail. I had a hard time recognizing them this way. I looked at their faces and they looked different. It was like seeing a movie star nude, no makeup, eyes small and blinking.

The fire girl started to shiver and she closed her eyes. She held on hard.

It's so much quieter like this, she murmured.

The other girl winced. Not for me, she said. Her face was beginning to flush a little.

The fire girl opened her eyes. No, she said, nodding, of course. It would be different for you.

I clasped my own hands together. I felt tepid. I felt out of my league.

I don't suppose I can hold your hand all day, the fire girl said in a low voice.

The ice girl shook her head. I have to be at the hospital, she said, I need my hand. She seemed uncomfortable. Her face was getting redder. She held on a second longer. I need my hand, she said. She let go.

The fire girl hung her head. Her hand blazed up in a second, twirling into turrets. I pictured her at the mountains again—that ribbon of pleasure, tasting Roy with her finger-tips.

Ice whirled back around the other girl's hand. She stepped back, and the color emptied out of her face.

It's awful, the fire girl said, shaking her wrist, sending sparks flying, starting to pace her cell. I want to burn every-thing. I want to burn *everything*. She gripped the iron frame of the cot until it glowed red under her palm. Do you under-stand? she said, it's all I think about.

We could cut it off, said the ice girl then.

We both stared at her.

Are you kidding? I said, you can't cut off the *fire* hand, it's a beautiful thing, it's a wonderful thing—

But the fire girl had released the bed and was up against the bars. Do you think it would work? she said. Do you think that would do something?

The ice girl shrugged. I don't know, she said, but it might be worth a try.

I wanted to give a protest here but I was no speechwriter; the speechwriter had left town forever and taken all the good speeches with him. I kept beginning sentences and dropping them off. Finally, they sent me out to find a knife. I don't know what they talked about while I was gone. I wasn't sure where to go so I just ran home, grabbed a huge sharp knife from the kitchen, and ran back. In ten minutes I was in the cell again, out of breath, the wooden knife handle tucked into my belt like a sword.

The fire girl was amazed. You're fast, she said. I felt flattered. I thought maybe I could be the fast girl. I was busy for a second renaming myself Atalanta when I looked over and saw how nervous and scared she was.

Don't do this, I said, you'll miss it.

But she'd already reached over and grabbed the knife and was pacing her cell again, flicking sparks onto the wall. She spoke mainly to herself. It would all be so much easier, she said.

The ice girl had no expression. I'll stay, she said, tightening her ponytail, in case you need healing. I wanted to kick her. There was a horrible ache growing in my stomach.

The fire girl took a deep breath. Then, kneeling down, she laid her hand, leaping with flames, on the stone jail floor and slammed the knife down right where the flesh of her wrist began. After sawing for a minute, she let out a shout and the hand separated and she ran over to the ice girl who put her healing bulb directly on the wound.

Tears streaked down the fire girl's face and she shifted her weight from foot to foot. The cut-off hand was hidden in a cloud of smoke on the floor. The ice girl leaned in, her soother face intent, but something strange was happening. The ice bulb wasn't working. There was no ice at all. The ice girl found herself with just a regular flesh hand, clasping the sawed-off tuber of a wrist. Equalized and normal. The fire girl looked down in horror.

Oh, pleaded the fire girl, never let go, *please,* don't, *please,* but it was too late. Her wrist had already been released to the air.

The fire girl's arm blazed up to the elbow. It was a bigger blaze now, a looser one, a less dexterous flame with no fingers to guide it. Oh no, she cried, trying to shake it off, oh *no.* The ice girl was silent, holding her hand as it reiced in her flesh palm, turning it slowly, numbing up. I was twisting in the corner, the ache in my stomach fading, trying to think of the right thing to say. But her body was now twice as burning and twice as loud and twice as powerful and twice everything. I still thought it was beautiful, but I was just an observer. The ice girl slipped silently down the hallway and I only stayed for a few more minutes. It was too hard to see. The fire girl started slamming her arm against the brick wall. When I left, she was sitting down with her chopped-off hand, burning it to pieces, one finger at a time.

They let her out a week later, but they made her strap her arm to a metal bucket of ice. The ice girl even dripped a few drops into it, to make it especially potent. The bucket would heat up on occasion but her arm apparently quieted. I didn't go to see her on the day she got out; I stayed at home. I felt responsible and ashamed: it was me who'd brought the ice girl to the jail, I'd fetched the knife, and worst, I was still *so* relieved it hadn't worked. Instead, I sat in my room at home that day and thought about J. in the Big City. He didn't give speeches about me anymore. Now we stood together in the middle of a busy street, dodging whizzing cars, and I'd pull him tight to me and begin to learn his skin.

All sorts of stories passed through the town about the fire girl on her day of release: She was covered in ash! She was all fire with one flesh hand! My personal favorite was that even her teeth were little flaming squares. The truth was, she found a shack in the back of town by the mountains, a shack made of metal, and she set up a home there.

The funny thing is what happened to the ice girl after all of it. She quit her job at the hospital, and she split. I thought I'd leave, I thought the fire girl would leave, but it was the ice girl who left. I passed her on the street the day before.

How are you doing, I said, how is the hospital?

She turned away from me, still couldn't look me in the eye. Everyone is sick in the hospital, she said. She stood there and I waited for her to continue. Do you realize, she said, that if I cut off my arm, my entire body might freeze?

Wow, I said. Think of all the people you could cure. I couldn't help it. I was still mad at her for suggesting the knife at all.

Yeah, she said, eyes flicking over to me for a second, think of that.

I watched her. I was remembering her face in the jail, waiting to see what would happen when the fire hand was removed. Hoping, I suppose, for a different outcome. I put my hands in my pockets. I guess I never told you, she said, but I feel nothing. I just feel ice.

I nodded. I wasn't surprised.

She turned a bit. I'm off now, she said, bye.

When the town discovered she had disappeared, there was a big uproar, and everybody blamed the fire girl. They thought she'd burned her up or something. The fire girl who never left her metal shack, sitting in her living room, her arm in that bucket. The whole town blamed her until a hungry nurse opened the hospital freezer and found one thousand Dixie cups filled with magic ice. They knew it was *her* ice because as soon as they brought a cup to a stroke patient, he improved and went home in two days. No one could figure it out, why the ice girl had left, but they stopped blaming the fire girl. Instead, they had an auction for the ice cups. People mortgaged their houses for one little cup; just in case, even if

132

everyone was healthy; just in case. This was a good thing to hoard in your freezer.

The ones who didn't get a cup went to the fire girl. When they were troubled, or lonely, or in pain, they went to see her. If they were lucky, she'd remove her blazing arm from the ice bucket and gently touch their faces with the point of her wrist. The burns healed slowly, leaving marks on their cheeks. There was a whole group of scar people who walked around town now. I asked them: Does it hurt? And the scar people nodded, yes. But it felt somehow wonderful, they said. For one long second, it felt like the world was holding them close.

LOSER

Once there was an orphan who had a knack for finding lost things. Both his parents had been killed when he was eight years old—they were swimming in the ocean when it turned wild with waves, and each had tried to save the other from drowning. The boy woke up from a nap, on the sand, alone. After the tragedy, the community adopted and raised him, and a few years after the deaths of his parents, he began to have a sense of objects even when they weren't visible. This ability continued growing in power through his teens and by his twenties, he was able to actually sniff out lost sunglasses, keys, contact lenses and sweaters.

The neighbors discovered his talent accidentally—he was over at Jenny Sugar's house one evening, picking her up for a date, when Jenny's mother misplaced her hairbrush, and was walking around, complaining about this. The young man's nose twitched and he turned slightly toward the kitchen and pointed to the drawer where the spoons and knives were kept. His date burst into laughter. Now that would be quite a silly place to put the brush, she said, among all that silverware! and she opened the drawer to make her point, to wave with a knife or brush her hair with a spoon, but when she did, boom, there was the hairbrush, matted with gray curls, sitting astride the fork pile.

Jenny's mother kissed the young man on the cheek but Jenny herself looked at him suspiciously all night long.

You planned all that, didn't you, she said, over dinner. You were trying to impress my mother. Well you didn't impress me, she said.

He tried to explain himself but she would hear none of it and when he drove his car up to her house, she fled before he could even finish saying he'd had a nice time, which was a lie anyway. He went home to his tiny room and thought about the word lonely and how it sounded and looked so lonely, with those two l's in it, each standing tall by itself.

As news spread around the neighborhood about the young man's skills, people reacted two ways: there were the deeply appreciative and the skeptics. The appreciative ones called up the young man regularly. He'd stop by on his way to school, find their keys, and they'd give him a homemade muffin. The skeptics called him over too, and watched him like a hawk; he'd still find their lost items but they'd insist it was an elaborate scam and he was doing it all to get attention. Maybe, declared one woman, waving her index finger in the air, Maybe, she said, he steals the thing so we think it's lost, moves the item, and then comes over to save it! How do we know it was really lost in the first place? What is going on?

The young man didn't know himself. All he knew was the feeling of a tug, light but insistent, like a child at his sleeve, and that tug would turn him in the right direction and show him where to look. Each object had its own way of inhabiting space, and therefore messaging its location. The young man could sense, could smell, an object's presence—he did not need to see it to feel where it put its gravity down. As would be expected, items that turned out to be miles away took much harder concentration than the ones that were two feet to the left.

When Mrs. Allen's little boy didn't come home one afternoon, that was the most difficult of all. Leonard Allen was eight years old and usually arrived home from school at 3:05. He had allergies and needed a pill before he went back out to play. That day, by 3:45, a lone Mrs. Allen was a wreck. Her boy rarely got lost—only once had that happened in the supermarket but he'd been found quite easily under the produce tables, crying; this walk home from school was a straight line and Leonard was not a wandering kind.

Mrs. Allen was just a regular neighbor except for one extraordinary fact—through an inheritance, she was the owner of a gargantuan emerald she called the Green Star. It sat, glass-cased, in her kitchen, where everyone could see it because she insisted that it be seen. Sometimes, as a party trick, she'd even cut steak with its beveled edge.

On this day, she removed the case off the Green Star and

stuck her palms on it. Where is my boy? she cried. The Green Star was cold and flat. She ran, weeping, to her neighbor, who calmly walked her back home; together, they gave the house a thorough search, and then the neighbor, a believer, recommended calling the young man. Although Mrs. Allen was a skeptic, she thought anything was a worthwhile idea, and when the line picked up, she said, in a trembling voice:

You must find my boy.

The young man had been just about to go play basketball with his friends. He'd located the basketball in the bathtub.

You lost him? said the young man.

Mrs. Allen began to explain and then her phone clicked.

One moment please, she said, and the young man held on. When her voice returned, it was shaking with rage.

He's been kidnapped! she said. And they want the Green Star!

The young man realized then it was Mrs. Allen he was talking to, and nodded. Oh, he said, I see. Everyone in town was familiar with Mrs. Allen's Green Star. I'll be right over, he said.

The woman's voice was too run with tears to respond.

In his basketball shorts and shirt, the young man jogged over to Mrs. Allen's house. He was amazed at how the Green Star was all exactly the same shade of green. He had a desire to lick it.

By then, Mrs. Allen was in hysterics.

They didn't tell me what to do, she sobbed. Where do I bring my emerald? How do I get my boy back?

The young man tried to feel the scent of the boy. He asked for a photograph and stared at it—a brown-haired kid at his kindergarten graduation—but the young man had only found objects before, and lost objects at that. He'd never found anything, or anybody, stolen. He wasn't a policeman.

Mrs. Allen called the police and one officer showed up at the door.

Oh it's the finding guy, the officer said. The young man dipped his head modestly. He turned to his right; to his left; north; south. He got a glimmer of a feeling toward the north and walked out the back door, through the backyard. Night approached and the sky seemed to grow and deepen in the darkness.

What's his name again? he called back to Mrs. Allen.

Leonard, she said. He heard the policeman pull out a pad and begin to ask basic questions.

He couldn't quite feel him. He felt the air and he felt the tug inside of the Green Star, an object displaced from its original home in Asia. He felt the tug of the tree in the front yard which had been uprooted from Virginia to be replanted here, and he felt the tug of his own watch which was from his uncle; in an attempt to be fatherly, his uncle had insisted he take it but they both knew the gesture was false.

Maybe the boy was too far away by now.

He heard the policeman ask: What is he wearing?

Mrs. Allen described a blue shirt, and the young man focused in on the blue shirt; he turned off his distractions and the blue shirt, like a connecting radio station, came calling from the northwest. The young man went walking and walking and about fourteen houses down he felt the blue shirt shrieking at him and he walked right into the backyard, through the back door, and sure enough, there were four people watching TV including the tear-stained boy with a runny nose eating a candy bar. The young man scooped up the boy while the others watched, so surprised they did nothing, and one even muttered: Sorry, man.

For fourteen houses back, the young man held Leonard in his arms like a bride. Leonard stopped sneezing and looked up at the stars and the young man smelled Leonard's hair, rich with the memory of peanut butter. He hoped Leonard would ask him a question, any question, but Leonard was quiet. The young man answered in his head: Son, he said, and the word rolled around, a marble on a marble floor. Son, he wanted to say.

When he reached Mrs. Allen's door, which was wide open, he walked in with quiet Leonard and Mrs. Allen promptly burst into tears and the policeman slunk out the door.

She thanked the young man a thousand times, even offered him the Green Star, but he refused it. Leonard turned on the TV and curled up on the sofa. The young man walked over and asked him about the program he was watching but Leonard stuck a thumb in his mouth and didn't respond.

Feel better, he said softly. Tucking the basketball beneath his arm, the young man walked home, shoulders low.

In his tiny room, he undressed and lay in bed. Had it been

a naked child with nothing on, no shoes, no necklace, no hairbow, no watch, he could not have found it. He lay in bed that night with the trees from other places rustling and he could feel their confusion. No snow here. Not a lot of rain. Where am I? What is wrong with this dirt?

Crossing his hands in front of himself, he held on to his shoulders. Concentrate hard, he thought. Where are you? Everything felt blank and quiet. He couldn't feel a tug. He squeezed his eyes shut and let the question bubble up: Where did you go? Come find me. I'm over here. Come find me.

If he listened hard enough, he thought he could hear the waves hitting.

LEGACY

The hunchback took in the pregnant girl to hide her from high school until the baby popped out. He was her stepuncle, stepmother's side, lived in a castle with a butler and several spoiled cats. Her parents, disturbed by the predicament, brewed over the problem until her father came up with the brilliant idea: That castle! Your weird brother! Wanting nothing more to do with their daughter, they placed her on a castle-bound train with a suitcase of wide-waisted dresses and a thank-you fern.

Chin brave, the girl ascended the four hundred stairs over the moat and decided she liked the view of the garden from her bedroom. The butler threw out the fern. She held her belly in her arms and bounced with it while the hunchback, a gourmet vegetarian, served her creamy spinach and mashed buttered yams in his cold, stone-walled kitchen.

By her fifth month, they were lovers. He licked her body

up, thirsted after her swollen breasts, consumed her corners until she felt she was one cohesive circle.

I never really came with *him,* she whispered one night to the hunchback, pointing to her stomach. Someone once told me that if the woman comes at conception, then the baby will be lucky. Let me tell you, she continued, if that's true, this'll be one cursed child.

The hunchback burst into laughter and held her tightly because just ten minutes before she could hardly *stop* coming from the insistent lappings of his tongue. He said Maybe some of our luck is going up, post-conception luck, and she sank into his millions of pillows and let out a breath of satisfaction. When they slept, she spooned him from behind, her extended belly fitting perfectly into the space created beneath the lurch of his hunch.

She dreamed about luck traveling up her inner thighs, sparkling and ticklish, like softened diamonds.

After the baby came, she wouldn't leave. No one called for her, and she wouldn't have gone with them anyway. She wanted to stay, she told him and he nodded. He said Move into my room and she did in two hours, his room with its strange swaybacked chairs and the midnight-blue four-poster bed. She was at his desk one morning, preparing the papers for the baby to be his, for him to be the official father, when she came across medical papers from a plastic surgery clinic. What's this she said out loud but the hunchback was in the

rose garden, weeding. She read the papers because she figured
This is to be my baby's father, and she found out that two
years previous this ordinary normal man had had a hump
added to his back. The doctors had opened up his skin and
injected fat globules into his shoulder region, and it had cost
him a lot of money but he was really rich. The papers said
Warning: overeating will affect the size of this hump which
explained to her the way it had swelled on Thanksgiving
night; she'd chalked it up to her own imagination.

You mean you're not for real? she screeched, and she ran
outside to the weeds while the baby slept and she poked at his
back hard until he said You're hurting me and she said You're
a fake fake fake! and scooping up the baby she flew down the
four hundred stairs. She walked the streets of the city until she
found a cheap apartment on the bad side of town. She met a
man with no legs. How did you get this way, she asked, and
he said My father didn't know I was under the car working
on it and she said I'm so sorry and took off her clothes. He
was not the lover that the hunchback was, though. She only
came every now and then when she allowed herself the re-
membrance of his hands and his tongue. She quieted and
took up nursing, specializing in deformities. But the baby: she
did turn out lucky. She grew up to be a movie star. She
headlined movies in silver dresses and everyone watched her
huge face on the screen with her long long eyelashes and said
This one is Special.

It was so unfortunate that her career ended the way it did. On the set of her fifth movie, the starlet was sitting at her makeup table with her head on her arms feeling inestimably sad. I have beauty and fame and riches and boyfriends, she thought, and yet I am so unhappy. Her mother, a frequent visitor, knocked at the door of the trailer. Sweetheart she said opening the door, they— She stopped in mid-sentence. She saw it right away. What's this? she gasped, face falling open, leaning on the door for support. The starlet raised her burdened head and looked at herself in the mirror. She saw the hump rising up on her back like a landscaped hill, and reaching back one tentative hand to touch it, could hardly contain the airborne feeling of relief.

DREAMING IN
POLISH

There was an old man and an old woman and they dreamed the same dreams. They'd been married for sixty years, and their arm skin now wrinkled down to their wrists like kicked-down bedsheets. They were maybe the oldest people in the world. They sat outside their house together, elbows touching, in the wicker chairs you'd expect them to sit in, and watched the people walk by. Occasionally they called out images from the night before to the gardener or to whoever happened to be passing. Most people smiled quickly at them and then looked back down at the sidewalk. And when night fell, the old man and the old woman walked into their bedroom, drew back the white sheets, covered themselves up, and shared what was beneath.

. . .

This summer was the one where I worked in the hardware store, and my mother talked only about going to Washington, D.C., to ride on the cattle cars at the newly inaugurated Holocaust Museum there. Apparently this museum had the best simulation of Auschwitz in the world. I didn't want to go; I was happy giving refunds to wives who'd bought the wrong pliers for their enterprising husbands. Besides, my mother and I had pretty much done the concentration-camp museum circuit by this point—looking at piles of hair in the Paris one the summer before, walking past black-and-white photographs in Amsterdam. I didn't like going, but she, somehow, craved it. I watched her hands tremble as she looked at the biographies pasted on the walls, and wondered what she was thinking.

My mother didn't have much to do with her day besides plan these trips; she taught, and kept her summers free, but I was very busy at the store, stacking bags of potting soil until they were all in perfect rows. I spent my afternoons scraping bird shit off a statue of a random Greek god that stood in the town's central square. The statue had ended up there inexplicably—no one, not even the oldest people, remembered when it arrived. It seemed to have simply grown up from the earth. My boss at the hardware store thought it was his duty to keep it shining, so every afternoon when business was quiet, he sent me outside, and I rubbed the dried white off muscled iron thighs, running my cloth down sinewy gray biceps. This was the only man I had ever touched so closely. I sang songs in my head from the Sunday morning countdown while I cleaned him. I kept songs going in my head because they were the easiest thing to think about.

At home, during the evenings, I took care of my father, who was sick and stayed in bed all day. My mother thought I made the better nurse. I told him all about my day, half-listening to my mother watching television in the next room, her wrist cracking and popping when she saw something she thought was funny. She did that instead of laughing.

My father liked to hear details about the store. He liked talking about hardware.

"Any wrenches back today?" he asked, arms flat by his sides, sticks.

"Yes," I replied. "Mrs. Johnson said hers was the wrong size, so we just traded that one in, and there was a man passing through who needed one for his car, he was having car trouble."

"Transmission," my father said knowingly, relaxing further into his pillow.

The old man and the old woman once dreamed that a pig drowned. As usual, they announced this to the neighborhood, listening closely to the sounds of their own voices. They rarely spoke in sentences, but instead called out the images in fragments, like young earnest poets.

"Pig," the old woman said.

"No breath," he finished.

"Pushing pig," she said.

"And brown and dead."

That day a farmer from across town heard them as he walked by, and when he arrived home his wife hurried out to tell him that the tractor had accidentally scooped up a pig instead of earth and thrown it headfirst into a pile of manure. The pig couldn't get its footing, fell forward, and suffocated. The farmer was disgusted and annoyed by the story but didn't think of the significance until he was on the toilet before he went to bed and then he remembered the old man and the old woman. And brown and dead. Disturbed, he told his wife about the prophets in the town, and she promptly told all the neighbors. When the news got back to them, the old man and the old woman just smiled and touched elbow bones closely, loose skin nearly obscuring the tattooed numbers on their inner arms.

I brought my father potting soil and put a pot of growing radishes by his bed so he would have something to tend to. He watered it maybe twenty times a day with an eyedropper, placing strategic drops near the roots—this would increase growth capacity, he said. And I told him plants grow more if you talk to them, so I'd find him, at odd hours in the day, whispering secrets into the damp dirt—about his dreams, about what it was like to be sick, I thought. About his first kiss and other stories.

But when I sat with him it was only me who would talk: Celia and her Anecdotes. He wanted to know, with a powerful urgency, what I did in fourth grade, because he'd been well then and hadn't paid attention to what I was doing. He was busy flying into enormous airports and doing deals. He dreamed, then, of having a son and playing catch on the lawn. Now I knew he thanked God he'd had a daughter. A son would be long gone. A son would be windswept in New York City, the warmth of red wine in his mouth, hands firm on voluptuous women while his father grew thinner and thinner in a queen-sized bed in the country.

I told my father about Reggie, the fat boy with a bowl cut that I liked in third grade and how I cried the day he moved to Kentucky, and I told my father about my former best friend Lonnie and how she had sex at fourteen, and how dumb that was of her. Fast-lane Lonnie. He settled himself back in the bed, and smiled as I talked. I could hear myself prattling, sounding so young and eager. I thought that if I were my father I would want to pat my head. Sure enough, when I kissed him good night, he rubbed my hair with his bony fingers, still steady and confident.

"You're a good girl, Celia," he said. "You're a little prize just waiting to be discovered."

"Oh," I said quickly, somewhat annoyed, "I'm not waiting for anything." Closing the door gently, I went into the kitchen and stared at things. Then I wiped the stove down until it waxed white and pearly under my cloth.

. . .

In the concentration-camp museum in Los Angeles you had to pretend you were a deportee, and choose between two doors: one for the young and healthy and another for feebler people that used to go straight to a gas chamber. I chose the "able-bodied" door and found myself in a stone room with twenty other Jews, all of us picking at our clothing. I didn't really understand why I was there, suffering through yet another museum, until I caught myself sending a hello to the ceiling. And then I knew I was visiting the dead people. I wanted to let them know I'd come back. That for some reason, no matter how much I wanted to, I couldn't leave them behind, loosened on the ceiling, like invisible sad smoke.

One day the old man and the old woman woke in a panic. They looked at each other and babbled something in Polish, the language they only used when they were scared. They rushed onto the porch and alerted a young gardener who was planting azaleas across the street.

"You," the old man cried. "Stop!"

The townspeople passing by, who revered the old man and the old woman as minor prophets due to the pig phenomenon, stopped and listened. The gardener wiped his dirty hands on the grass. The old woman was spluttering, her body stooped and visible through a soft yellow nightgown.

"No other gods before me. Or we're all dead. Town will die, die, die!" she cried shrilly, then fell back into her wicker chair.

The townspeople were instantly alarmed by the prophecy. They ran to the mayor who listened with studied concentration, stared at the floor, and then spoke.

"Town meeting," he announced in a firm, authoritative voice previously used only for the dog when it peed on the carpet. "We must hold a town meeting."

In a flurry, the townspeople were assembled. The gardener paraphrased what he'd heard. " 'No other gods before me or we're all dead, dead, dead,' she said." Due to all the anxiety, no one could really make any sense of the obvious until Sylvie Johnson, a Catholic who owned the potato store (all kinds— red, white, brown), spoke up.

"It's Commandment Two," she said calmly, pleased to demonstrate her Bible knowledge.

The crowd murmured in both recognition and feigned recognition.

"What do they mean by dead?" asked an older banker.

Everyone looked up at the mayor for some guidance.

"Hmmm," he said. "Hmmm." He looked out over the people. "Just follow it." He was humbled by the possible presence of God in his congregation. "Town dismissed."

Everyone streamed out of the gymnasium. By nightfall, garbage bins all over the city were overflowing with sculptures from Africa and colorful masks from Mexico, anything that even slightly resembled Another God Before Him. There was much concern over the Greek god statue in the park; its base was wedged several feet into the ground, and therefore extremely difficult to move. Finally the mayor draped a white sheet over it, which seemed to satisfy the worried public. It looked like a piece of long-awaited artwork, waiting to be revealed.

My mother began taking long walks to nowhere. She would leave the house in the afternoon and call me two or three hours later from a phone booth. I would drive and get her. When we returned home, she would go straight into my father's room and for ten minutes she would love him beautifully, holding his cheeks, playing melodies on his hair.

I often wanted to be like my mother because she had long hair with red in it and to me that proved she was crackling inside. Somewhere in her there was a gene of impulsiveness, a gene I was sure I lacked. My hair was brown; at times I would dye it temporarily red for a week but it felt like putting a princess's gown on a handmaid. The breeding was not there.

Once when the sunset light came into the living room, my hair did turn red, really red, like my mother's. I watched it set my head on fire for several minutes, holding up strands and letting them fall. I felt I was in another country, where the air was so hot you could see it, and my back was dripping with sweat. I felt, for an instant, the absurd sturdiness of my legs and my back. Then I heard my dad in the other room, counting the drops under his breath as he watered the radishes, and I went to take a shower, to erase the red from my hair. I scrubbed my body fiercely with the soap, as if it were not mine, as if it weren't young, or soft, or wondering. I tried to imagine what it would be like not to want things. I tried to empty all the things I wanted into the drain and let them swirl away from me, silenced.

I came home from the store one afternoon and found my father had fallen out of bed onto the floor. He'd had some sort of seizure because his sheets were twisted into ropes near his feet and the radishes were broken on the carpet, a pile of dirt and terra cotta. My mother was on a walk. I rushed to the phone and looked at it, then rushed back to him. He was breathing, I could see that, but his head was strangely tilted and he didn't respond when I said his name. I said his name a few times anyway, but I didn't want to touch him. I could see the strange black hairs on his thighs that were usually hidden by the yellow blanket. I stepped into the backyard and ran and ran little tight circles around the lemon tree, leaning my head in to increase the centripetal force, trusting this would prevent me from running away. I wondered if there was a train waiting at the train station, going to someplace beautiful; I wondered if the conductor had a mistress that he kept in the caboose. I imagined him stepping through the cars to reach her, train shaking, going to see her, going to make love to her in the shaking long train, and I kept making the train longer, pushing him back, ten cars, twenty cars, an impossible length before he can see her, and I pushed him and pushed him until

I heard my mother open the front door. She went straight into my father's room. Running inside, I found her kneeling at his body, a hand on his leg, taking a pulse.

"Celia," she said. She was clutching a brown bag from the bookstore. I wondered what she'd bought.

"Here," I said.

She looked up at me. "Help me lift him up," she said. "He's okay."

Once he was in bed, he looked normal, like a regular sleeping person. My mother made me a hamburger and we watched TV for five hours. It was Tuesday night, a reasonably good TV night, which was lucky. Before I went to bed, I wandered briefly into my father's room; his breathing was calm. I stopped and fingered a baby radish buried in the mess on the floor. It was hard and red as a reptile's heart.

The old man and the old woman still dreamed the same dreams but she could no longer speak anything but Polish. Regardless, there were usually at least eight or nine devout followers sitting in front of their house, listening. As a whole, the town was now alert, on edge. Nervous about the commandment, people went about their day with great caution, trying hard not to make the irreparable goof. There was a moment of terror in the hardware store when Mrs. Johnson accidentally blurted, "Oh my stars," after dropping a wrench on her foot. Everyone held their breath and wondered if it was the end. Nothing did actually happen, but Mrs. Johnson hurried home in a daze, and parents hugged their children a little closer than usual that evening at bedtime.

The old woman loved her audience, and didn't seem to realize that no one understood her anymore. She asked the gardener long complicated questions in Polish. But since his parents were immigrants too, he always nodded appropriately, and often picked a flower from the garden and gave it to her before he left. The old woman placed the flower in the hand she always shared with her husband, and they sat, quiet and patient, fingertips linked by the bloom.

One afternoon my mother went on a walk and didn't come back. By nine o'clock my father seemed confused because he kept asking me if the TV was on. An on TV was a sure sign that my mother was home. After a while I just turned it on anyway even though he could tell from his room that it was alone, blaring to an empty couch, a lamp turned off.

By eleven, I was worried and drove by the bookstore looking for her familiar turned-out walk. There was no one but people my age, weaving through the sidewalk, heads on shoulders, the taste of beer in their mouths. I imagined fast-lane Lonnie, out with her boyfriend, her hand calm on the small of his back; I imagined my mother in Niagara Falls, screaming and laughing into crashes of bluish water.

When I got home my father was nearly asleep. He heard the front door and called out from the darkness.

"Ellen," he said.

"Celia."

"Don't worry, sweetie," he said. "She just does these things sometimes. Tomorrow."

"I should call the police," I said.

"No," he said firmly, "really. If by tomorrow this time we've no news, then okay. But she'll call."

I smiled. I knew he was wrong. But as a comfort, I stayed in the living room with the TV on all night, as she often did. I didn't really watch much, but stared at the reflected silhouette of my body in the TV screen, twirling my ankle sometimes just to remind myself that I was there.

The next night after dinner we still hadn't heard a word. I brought him milk and sat by his bed.

"She'll call," I said feebly.

"I know," he said. "She just does this sometimes."

"Yeah," I said.

"Really." He looked at me for a moment, touched my hair with his forefinger. "You're a pretty girl, my Celia," he said. "You ought to go out sometimes. You must be so sick of taking care of me."

"No," I said, trying to think of something to say. "No."

"Boys, any boys you like now?" he asked.

"No," I said again. "No boys." He looked at me and patted my head again. I could feel myself smile.

. . .

She called at ten. She was at a bar in Connecticut, on her way to D.C., to the museum, walking. She had a day or so more to go, and she wanted me to send my father on a train, bundled in blankets to keep him warm. She wanted him to meet her; they could go on the cattle cars together. She said her feet were already very blistered, and I imagined her relaxing into the cattle car, arm around my blanketed father as they prepared to experience simulated genocide.

"Put your father on the phone," my mother told me.

"He's asleep," I said. "We were both really worried. You didn't call. I was sure—we didn't know where you were."

"Is that Ellen?" I heard my father's voice, oddly strong, from his room.

"Put him on," my mom said.

"He's tired," I said.

"Celia," she ordered. "Now."

I brought him to the phone. He was delighted to hear her voice. I waited for him to be angry, to tell her how mad we were, but he didn't sound angry at all. Instead, he curled up in his bed like a teenage girl, and cooed into the receiver. I walked, disgusted, into the living room, and watched my ankle in the TV again until I heard the click.

"She wants me to take a train and meet her in D.C.," he said.

"Oh well," I said.

"But if I'm bundled up and in a wheelchair I should be okay," he said. "You know, we'll explain it to the conductor. It'd be fun to go on a trip."

159

"Are you kidding?" I asked.

"No," he said, "no, it could work. It's a little crazy, I know, but it could work. Your mother is walking to Washington—now *that* is crazy."

I stared at him. "It'll give you a break," he said. "You can have a little vacation from us."

I wasn't sure if he'd suddenly lost his mind. He'd been in bed for several months. He hadn't been outside for an entire season.

"Daddy?" I asked.

"I'll take a lot of vitamin C," he said. "It'll be fine. I'll go tomorrow. You'll take me to the train station?"

I walked to the door frame of his room and looked at him, so thin under the many blankets that I couldn't see his body anymore.

"Really, Celia," he said, "I wouldn't try if I didn't think I could do it."

"Let's see in the morning," I said quietly. He smiled at me and clicked off his light. I stayed in the door frame for a few minutes, trying only to remember the words of radio songs, trying hard to fill my whole brain with hundreds and hundreds of lyrics. I cleaned the refrigerator but it was clean. Finally I left the house.

The night was warm and clear, all the lights off in the neighborhood, front lawns wide and empty. I walked through the streets counting the sidewalk squares over and over under my feet until I reached one thousand, which brought me right to the middle of the center square. And there was the

Greek statue looming under its sheet. I stood quietly at its base, and looked around. The park was empty, only trees and circles of splintering wooden benches surrounding me. Even under the sheet, the statue commanded the space. I began to run in front of it, back and forth in tight rows.

"I'm going to do something," I warned, back and forth in front of the pedestal. Windows in the distance were dark, people sleeping, holding their wishes in tightly. I could hear my breath mounting as I ran faster. "I'm going to show him," I yelled, louder this time. The silence was great and empty. I ran for a moment more, faster, faster, then stopped abruptly in front of the base of the statue, and stilled my body. Breathing quickly, I grabbed a corner of the white sheet. I rubbed the corner over and over between my fingers, chafing my skin, until it climbed into my fist and I had a good hold. And then, with one fierce yank, I pulled the sheet off. It blew up high, like a gasp, then floated to the ground, collapsing and bowing behind the statue.

Uncovered, the god looked huger than ever—young, unbreakable. I put my foot on the top of the pedestal and pulled myself up. I climbed on his foot, then his knee, until I was high enough to face him. Holding on to his shoulders to steady myself, I moved in close, arms wrapping around his shoulders, pressing into his chest.

"Father," I whispered. I listened as my breathing slowed, and waited for something to change.

THE RING

I fell in love with a robber and he took me on his rounds.

Don't talk too much, he said, or you'll mess me up.

As I talk a lot, this was difficult for me. He told me in a hushed voice to look around the kitchen while he went to scour under the living room couch. I stuck my hand in the flour canister and found a diamond ring! It was so hard not to shout out! Clamping a hand over my mouth, I whispered to my palm the word *diamond* over and over. I put it on my wedding finger and the white dust sprinkled over my glove as if someone was about to cook me.

The robber returned with a bag full of loot—three gold chains, a watch, two diamond bracelets and a shiny spoon—but when he saw that ring standing tall on my leather finger he proposed to me right then and there—took it off my finger, put it on again, kneeled down, looked me in the eye. And right there in a stranger's kitchen I said yes to that robber and both of our eyes filled with tears at the rightness of it all. Shutting the front door quietly behind us, we walked hand in hand to the car; when he said we were far enough away, I let out a shout of joy.

The next day we declared ourselves married and for our wedding night he went to the supermarket and bought ten bags of flour. Pouring it on my bedroom floor, my robber made a foot-deep flour sandbox. It was going to be a pain to vacuum but I loved the clean way it rolled off our skin and how I squeaked on the grains and when we kissed it tasted like morning.

Late that night I called my parents and told them I was married and my mother shrieked with delight and when my father asked: What does he do? I said, He's a baker. I could hear they were skeptical about the life of a baker's wife but I said, It's a good life and I love him and my mother said, That's all that's important, Penny—congratulations and my father grunted but I knew he was happy; I know his spectrum of grunts and this one was pleased.

We moved into a little apartment together on the rich side of town which was a good career choice for him. We used my furniture because he said he didn't have any. I got wedding gifts from my side of the family: a rainbow array of pot holders, a fluffy towel set, a million cashews. He didn't get anything from his family and he said that's because he didn't have one. Really, I said, why didn't I know that, and he said: Probably because I didn't tell you. I stood still for a second, absorbing this. He said, I don't own anything, Penny, family or furniture, and I piped in, You own me now! and he smiled and kissed the top of my head.

Handing me my dainty pair of black leather gloves, he donned his and said: Worktime, my lady, and I took his leather hand in my leather hand and squeezed it because I was now his family and we went four blocks down to the opera couple's mansion who were at that moment seeing *La Bohème* without us.

We crept alongside the house until we reached the kitchen window which was always open. My gentlemanly robber let me climb in first, and I blossomed into this new kitchen and did a quick twirl on the tile, imagining myself there cooking. I'd make a stew, I'd make lasagna. I'd make chocolate out of nothing but brown rice and water. Reaching out a hand, I lifted him in too and we stood for a moment in that first beautiful silence of takeover. I felt like the walls were bending to us. Then I got that curious urge and so we explored quickly; I found the bathroom with its big Art Deco black-and-red mirror and beckoned for him to come look with me. We gazed at our reflection together and I felt we looked like a particularly in-love couple in this particular mirror. I could tell he was itching to get under that living room couch, so I kissed him quickly and let him go hunt for gold while I returned to the kitchen and took to petting the very soft white cat. I checked the sugar this time, why not, and what do you know—down deep in the sugar canister was another ring, this time a ruby, the stone redder than the skin off cherries. I slipped it on over my glove and when my love came back with his bag of goods I showed it to him and he whirled me around in the air, right there next to someone else's oven. He told me he loved me and I blushed, the ring's sister. Before we left, he asked if I wanted to steal the cat too, but I said, No, you can't steal a cat, it's against the rules. It has a collar, it has a name; it belongs to them. While he crawled out the window, I made clicking sounds with my tongue to tell it goodbye and it leapt up on the sink to watch me leave, blue eyes unblinking.

That night, he sprinkled some sugar on our living room floor and we made love in it, dressed only in gloves and shoes; I lapped the sugar off his shoulder like a kitten. Sweet as it was, I had a hard time really being there with him that night because I kept stealing looks at that ring. It was so bright and so dark at the exact same time. After we were done, he went to take a shower and wash off the leftover sugar, and I pulled the ring off my glove and put it in Aunt Lula's sugar jar. When I went later to peek again at its crimson glory, I was surprised to find that the sugar was red too.

What? I said, Sweetie, did you pour fruit juice into the sugar jar?

He stirred and said, No, come back to bed, and I said, Wait just a second and put the ring in the flour.

Odd: in the morning, all the flour was red too. Red flour looks wrong.

Sweetie, I said, this ring is leaking, and I put it out on the counter and the counter turned red and I covered it up with a paper towel and the paper towel turned red and yes, even the tip of my finger was red now; I ran it under the tap but the water did nothing at all but get me wet.

My robber came out of the shower and I said: Sweetie, this ring has to go back or everything we own including ourselves will turn ruby and the robber picked it up with the gift towel from around his waist and the whole towel turned red and he said, Wow, you're right, okay.

That night the opera couple was out seeing *The Magic Flute* and we dropped the ring from a little paper bag that was of course red into their sugar jar again. Their sugar did not turn red and I couldn't figure that out. It seemed like there was something special about their sugar and it made me feel a little bit bad, like my sugar wasn't tough enough. Still, I kept lifting up the lid of the jar to see the ring nestled in there—it looked so beautiful glistening on the sugar crystals. The cat came to look with me and I wanted the cat badly but I knew that even if we took it home and gave it milk and renamed it, I still wouldn't feel like it was mine.

We jimmied the back door of the neighboring house; the couple was out of town somewhere cold. I'd watched them board the shuttle for the airport and he'd been wearing a ridiculous fur hat.

What did I go for this time? I went for the huge container of salt they had on their kitchen counter, the grandpapa of all salt shakers, and sure enough in there was a ring with an emerald the color of grass seen by someone with green eyes.

My sweetie hugged me and wanted to do it right there on the counter with the salt but I said I didn't want to make love in salt because it made me feel like dinner, in a bad way, and he said he understood.

We took the ring home and I put it in our salt and woke up in the middle of the night to see if our salt was green but it wasn't.

I climbed back into bed. It's still there, I whispered, and the salt is still salt.

He kissed my ear. Penny, he said, let's go to Tahiti and call it quits until winter again. I'm tired for now, let's get some sun. I said all right and he nestled his head into my shoulder. I looked at the diamond ring in the darkness, my little captured star, and I crept out of bed and went to the salt canister and retrieved the emerald ring and put it on my other hand. Climbing back into bed, I curled up to him again. The rings looked so beautiful together. I wanted three.

I guess I miss the other ring, I said out loud, though he seemed to be asleep.

When we got to Tahiti, in our pretty hotel room with the lavishly floral bedspreads and toilet paper folded into a point, he gave me a little wrapped gift in red wrapping paper and a beautiful red bow and I opened it up and I guess he'd not been asleep after all because what was it? It was that ruby ring.

Oh darling, oh sweetie, I said and I wanted to slip it on and I saw he'd attached a little rubber strip around the interior so that my hand wouldn't change. I noticed his fingertips were red from doing that, and I kissed him for his kindness. The ring caught the light like an open wound and I watched the sparkles all over my fingers dancing from red to green to white and back again and thought: I am the most stunning and loved baker's wife to ever live in the world ever.

We went swimming one hour after lunch. I was a little drunk from the second piña colada. The ruby ring slipped off my finger into the water. The ocean turned red.

All the swimmers ran out screaming. They thought it was blood, a massive hemorrhage by some very large person. I groped for the ring but got only handfuls of water. As far as the eye could see the ocean glistened scarlet, and in some places, it was even an electric magenta.

My robber paled and started to cry. This is the ocean, he said, what did you do, and I said, I forgot, and he said This is awful, throw in the green ring and I said But the salt stayed salt, and he said: Do it. So I did, I took the green ring off my finger and tossed it just under the arc of a little crimson wave. Nothing happened. The robber kept crying. I grew up by the sea, he said, I love blue, and he said Try the wedding ring and I said Our wedding ring? Our Wedding Ring? and he said You must and so I did, I tipped my hand down and just let it slide off my finger, cut past the surface of the waves and ring it, a full finger of water inside as it shimmied all the way down to the bottom of the sea. I heard him let out his breath when the ocean didn't change back. My fingers were bare and I could hardly recognize my own hands.

Now I started to cry. My marriage ring had been eaten by the huge red wet mouth of the ocean.

The robber stood crying and I stood crying and the sand glowed a pale orange. The environmental committee was already arriving in big trucks, with equipment. They were almost crying, it seemed, but they used megaphones to cover up the shaking in their voices. Check the fish, they called, and they did and the fish seemed fine. They measured the red part. I'd been fearing that the whole world's oceans were red now, but they said in their megaphone that the bleeding stopped one mile out. It was a one-mile ring. It was not all-powerful.

The robber and I went back to the hotel room. I sat in the bathroom and folded the toilet paper into a point like I worked there. When I went into the bedroom, he said he wanted to make love on sheets. I said No. He said Are you still mine? I still love you, do you love me? and I said I don't even know your first name, and for that matter, I don't know your last name either and besides, you just let our love plop into the ocean and so how am I supposed to love you now? I put my hands on my hips.

He said It wasn't our love that plopped into the ocean, Penny, it was just the ring, and I said But this was the ring from the flour jar and I don't know how to be yours without it.

He held my face in his hands. I looked out past the window to the foam crashing. It was pink.

Listen, I told him. I'm confused. I'm going home.

I took a shuttle to the Tahiti airport by myself. I left the robber sitting on the made bed, staring at the wall. I sat in the back of the shuttle bus and didn't talk except in curt one-word answers and the shuttle driver kept asking me questions that required more than one-word answers and he kept calling me Sugar and I was getting more and more annoyed and wanted to yank the steering wheel out of his hands and throw it out the window until out of the blue he gave me an idea. I barely remember paying him because I thought about this idea from the moment it came to me, and I thought about it the whole plane ride, through the snack and through the movie and through the dinner, and that's where I went first. I didn't even stop home to drop off my bags.

The white cat was still there and purred the second I touched it but more important, the sugar jar was still there too. I took it in my lap, opened the lid and peeked inside. The grains glittered.

Oh sugar, I said into it. You are the strongest of all.

I picked up their phone—it was a tortoiseshell phone with gold buttons—and called direct to the hotel room in Tahiti. To my surprise, the clerk said we had checked out several hours ago and just then there was a rattle at the window and in stepped the robber.

How did you know? I beamed, phone receiver in hand, and he shrugged, face tired and sunburned.

It was a good guess, he said. *Madame Butterfly* signs out and all.

We leaned forward and had an awkward hug. I held on to his elbow. He nudged his chin into my neck.

Pulling away, I held up the jar. So look at this, I said. Maybe this will help things.

What is it? he asked.

It's that special sugar.

Oh, he said. Well. I've always liked sugar.

I felt a little nervous but he gave me a good supportive look, so I dipped a finger into the sugar and licked it off. Mmm, I said, mmm, you've gotta try this. The grains sparkled on my tongue. The robber sat down in one of the wicker kitchen chairs next to me.

It's really good, I said.

He dipped in his own leathered finger and took a tentative lick off the glove. I watched his expression carefully. The house seemed very quiet except for the precise ticking of the clock above the kitchen table.

Do you feel any different? I asked.

Not yet, he said.

He put his finger in it again and I did too and once we touched fingertips and he curled his knuckle around mine and squeezed.

Hello there, I said softly, to our fingers.

He put his hand on my leg. My leg leaned into his hand.

I think we should eat it all, I stated. He moved closer to me. I'm full, he said. Keep eating, I said.

But Penny, it tastes just like regular sugar, he whispered into my ear.

Sshh, I murmured back, touching my shoulder to his, scooping up a new pile of grains into my hand. Don't tell.

THE GIRL IN THE

FLAMMABLE SKIRT

When I came home from school for lunch my father was wearing a backpack made of stone.

Take that off, I told him, that's far too heavy for you.

So he gave it to me.

It was solid rock. And dense, pushed out to its limit, gray and cold to the touch. Even the little zipper handle was made of stone and weighed a ton. I hunched over from the bulk and couldn't sit down because it didn't work with chairs very well so I stood, bent, in a corner, while my father whistled, wheeling about the house, relaxed and light and lovely now.

What's in this? I said, but he didn't hear me, he was changing channels.

I went into the TV room.

What's in this? I asked. This is so heavy. Why is it stone? Where did you get it?

He looked up at me. It's this thing I own, he said.

Can't we just put it down somewhere, I asked, can't we just sit it in the corner?

No, he said, this backpack must be worn. That's the law.

I squatted on the floor to even out the weight. What law? I asked. I never heard of this law before.

Trust me, he said, I know what I'm talking about. He did a few shoulder rolls and turned to look at me. Aren't you supposed to be in school? he asked.

I slogged back to school with it on and smushed myself and the backpack into a desk and the teacher sat down beside me while the other kids were doing their math.

It's so heavy, I said, everything feels very heavy right now.

She brought me a Kleenex.

I'm not crying, I told her.

I know, she said, touching my wrist. I just wanted to show you something light.

Here's something I picked up:

Two rats are hanging out in a labyrinth.

One rat is holding his belly. Man, he says, I am in so much pain. I ate all those sweet little sugar piles they gave us and now I have a bump on my stomach the size of my head. He turns on his side and shows the other rat the bulge.

The other rat nods sympathetically. Ow, she says.

The first rat cocks his head and squints a little. Hey, he says, did you eat that sweet stuff too?

The second rat nods.

The first rat twitches his nose. I don't get it, he says, look at you. You look robust and aglow, you don't look sick at all, you look bump-free and gorgeous, you look swinging and sleek. You look plain great! And you say you ate it too?

The second rat nods again.

Then how did you stay so fine? asks the first rat, touching his distended belly with a tiny claw.

I didn't, says the second rat. I'm the dog.

My hands were sweating. I wiped them flat on my thighs.

Then, ahem, I cleared my throat in front of my father. He looked up from his salad. I love you more than salt, I said.

He seemed touched, but he was a heart attack man and had given up salt two years before. It didn't mean *that* much to him, this ranking of mine. In fact, "Bland is a state of mind" was a favorite motto of his these days. Maybe you should give it up too, he said. No more french fries.

But I didn't have the heart attack, I said. Remember? That was you.

In addition to his weak heart my father also has weak legs so he uses a wheelchair to get around. He asked me to sit in a chair with him once, to try it out for a day.

But my chair doesn't have wheels, I told him. My chair just sits here.

That's true, he said, doing wheelies around the living room, that makes me feel really swift.

I sat in the chair for an entire afternoon. I started to get jittery. I started to do that thing I do with my hands, that knocking-on-wood thing. I was knocking against the chair leg for at least an hour, protecting the world that way, superhero me, saving the world from all my horrible and dangerous thoughts when my dad glared at me.

Stop that knocking! he said. That is really annoying.

I have to go to the bathroom, I said, glued to my seat.

Go right ahead, he said, what's keeping you. He rolled forward and turned on the TV.

I stood up. My knees felt shaky. The bathroom smelled very clean and the tile sparkled and I considered making it into my new bedroom. There is nothing soft in the bathroom. Everything in the bathroom is hard. It's shiny and new; it's scrubbed down and whited out; it's a palace of bleach and all you need is one fierce sponge and you can rub all the dirt away.

I washed my hands with a little duck soap and peered out the bathroom window. We live in a high-rise apartment building and often I wonder what would happen if there was a fire, no elevator allowed, and we had to evacuate. Who would carry him? Would I? Once I imagined taking him to the turning stairway and just dropping him down the middle chute, my mother at the bottom with her arms spread wide to catch his whistling body. Hey, I'd yell, catch Dad! Then I'd trip down the stairs like a little pony and find them both splayed out like car accident victims at the bottom and that's where the fantasy ends and usually where my knocking-on-wood hand starts to act up.

. . .

Paul's parents are alcoholics and drunk all the time so they don't notice that he's never home. Perhaps they conjure him up, visions of Paul, through their bleary whiskey eyes. But Paul is with me. I have locked Paul in my closet. Paul is my loverboy, sweet Paul is my olive.

I open the closet door a crack and pass him food. He slips the dirty plates from the last meal back to me and I stack them on the floor next to my T-shirts. Crouched outside the closet, I listen to him crunch and swallow.

How is it? I ask. What do you think of the salt-free meatball?

Paul says he loves sitting in the dark. He says my house is so quiet and it smells sober. The reason it's so quiet is because my father feels awful and is resting in his bedroom. Tiptoe, tiptoe round the sick papa. The reason it smells sober is because it is *so* sober. I haven't made a joke in this house in ten years at least. Ten years ago, I tried a Helen Keller joke on my parents and they sent me to my room for my terrible insensitivity to suffering.

I imagine in Paul's house everyone is running around in their underwear, and the air is so thick with bourbon your skin tans from it. He says no; he says the truth is his house is quiet also. But it's a more pointy silence, he says. A lighter one with sharper pricks. I nod and listen. He says too that in his house there are moisture rings making Olympian patterns on every possible wooden surface.

Once instead of food I pass my hand through the crack. He holds it for at least a half hour, brushing his fingers over my fingers and tracing the lines in my palm.

You have a long lifeline, he says.

Shut up, I tell him, I do not.

He doesn't let go of my hand, even then. Any dessert?

I produce a cookie out of my front shirt pocket.

He pulls my hand in closer. My shoulder crashes against the closet frame.

Come inside, he says, come join me.

I can't, I say, I need to stay out here.

Why? He is kissing my hand now. His lips are very soft and a little bit crumby.

I just do, I say, in case of an emergency. I think: because now I've learned my lesson and I'm terribly sensitive to suffering. Poor poor Helen K, blind-and-deaf-and-dumb. Because now I'm so sensitive I can hardly move.

Paul puts down his plate and brings his face up close to mine. He is looking right at me and I'm rustling inside. I don't look away. I want to cut off my head.

It is hard to kiss. As soon as I turn my head to kiss deeper, the closet door gets in the way.

After a minute Paul shoves the door open and pulls me inside with him. He closes the door back and now it is pitch black. I can feel his breath near mine, I can feel the air thickening between us.

I start shaking all over.

It's okay, he says, kissing my neck and my shoulder and my chin and more. He lets me out when I start to cry.

My father is in the hospital on his deathbed.

Darling, he says, you are my only child, my only heir.

To what? I ask. Is there a secret fortune?

No, he says, but you will carry on my genes.

I imagine several bedridden, wheelchaired children. I imagine throwing all my children in the garbage can because they don't work. I imagine a few more bad things and then I'm knocking on his nightstand and he's annoyed again.

Stop that noise, he says, I'm a dying man.

He grimaces in agony. He doesn't die though. This has happened a few times before and he never dies. The whole deathbed scene gets a little confusing when you play it out more than twice. It gets a bit hard to be sincere. At the hospital, I pray a lot, each time I pray with gusto, but my prayers are getting very strained; lately I have to grit my teeth. I picture his smiling face when I pray. I push that face into my head. Three times now when I picture this smiling face it explodes. Then I have to pray twice as hard. In the little hospital church I am the only one praying with my jaw clenched and my hands in fists knocking on the pew. Maybe they think I'm knocking on God's door, tap tap tap. Maybe I am.

When I'm done, I go out a side door into the day. The sky

is very hot and the hospital looks dingy in the sunlight and there is an outdoor janitorial supply closet with a hole in the bottom, and two rats are poking out of the hole and all I can see are their moving noses and I want to kick them but they're tucked behind the door. I think of bubonic plague. I think about rabies. I have half a bagel in my pocket from the hospital cafeteria and the rats can probably smell it; their little noses keep moving up and down frantically; I can tell they're hungry. I put my hand in my pocket and bring out the bagel but I just hold it there, in the air. It's cinnamon raisin. It smells like pocket lint. The rats don't come forward. They are trying to be polite. No one is around and I'm by the side of the hospital and it's late afternoon and I'm scot-free and young in the world. I am as breezy and light as a wing made from tissue paper. I don't know what to do with myself so I keep holding on tight to that bagel and sit down by the closet door. Where is my father already? I want him to come rolling out and hand over that knapsack of his; my back is breaking without it.

I think of that girl I read about in the paper—the one with the flammable skirt. She'd bought a rayon chiffon skirt, purple with wavy lines all over it. She wore it to a party and was dancing, too close to the vanilla-smelling candles, and suddenly she lit up like a pine needle torch. When the boy dancing next to her felt the heat and smelled the plasticky smell, he screamed and rolled the burning girl up in the carpet. She got third-degree burns up and down her thighs. But what I keep wondering about is this: that first second when she felt her skirt burning, what did she think? Before she knew it was the candles, did she think she'd done it herself? With the amazing turns of her hips, and the warmth of the music inside her, did she believe, for even one glorious second, that her passion had arrived?

ACKNOWLEDGMENTS

I'm so pleased and thankful to be able to publicly acknowledge the following people:

The UC–Irvine workshop was instrumental in helping me shape and form these stories, especially Cullen Gerst for his forthright and giving nature, Glen Gold for his storytelling convictions, Phil Hay for his stubbornly wise opinions about what fiction is, and Alice Sebold for her humor, strength, and friendship. Geoffrey Wolff offered tremendous encouragement and help in the true spirit of generous leadership, and I'm so grateful to Judith Grossman both for her aesthetic and for giving me that crucial second look.

Many thanks to my enthusiastic and intelligent editor, Bill Thomas, and to my agent, Henry Dunow, who is that excellent combination of thoughtfulness and warmth.

I am indebted to the journals that accepted my stories, and to those editors who encouraged me over time.

The outstanding Miranda Hoffman read nearly everything first, and from the beginning, has had a crucial unflagging belief in me. And this book itself is one of the triumphs of the work I did with Jeanne Burns Leary, and I am so grateful to her for her help in reminding me and teaching me and rereminding me and reteaching me that eagles don't catch flies.

Finally, my family: my parents, Meri and David Bender, with their mutual belief in the bizarre beauty of the unconscious, my gentle, powerhouse sisters, Suzanne and Karen, and my elegant fairy-tale-loving grandmother Ardie, have all in their own way both supported and inspired me by who they are, what they believe in, and by the sustaining strength of their love.